D0467481

SAMMY FERAL'S DIARIES OF

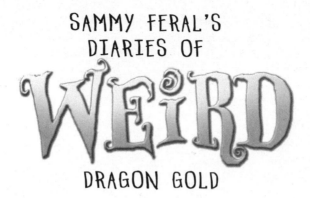

DRAGON GOLD

Books by Eleanor Hawken

Sammy Feral's Diaries of Weird
Sammy Feral's Diaries of Weird: Yeti Rescue
Sammy Feral's Diaries of Weird: Hell Hound Curse

Want to find out more about Eleanor?
Visit www.eleanorhawken.com for news, events and more!

SAMMY FERAL'S DIARIES OF

WEiRD

Dragon Gold

Eleanor Hawken

Illustrations by John Kelly

Quercus
New York • London

For Dylan, my greatest story yet.

Quercus

New York • London

Text © 2014 by Eleanor Hawken
Illustrations © 2014 by John Kelly

First published in the United States by Quercus in 2015

ISBN 978-1-62365-896-0

Library of Congress Control Number: 2014957509

Distributed in the United States and Canada by
Hachette Book Group
1290 Avenue of the Americas
New York, NY 10104

Manufactured in the United States

2 4 6 8 10 9 7 5 3 1

www.quercus.com

Monday, February 23

My mom has finally lost it. She's gone as crazy as a karaoke-singing kangaroo. She's not sleeping, she's not eating, she's wearing her clothes back to front and inside out, and her shoes on the wrong feet. She hasn't brushed her hair in days—there was a blackbird following her to the zoo this morning, and I'm pretty sure he was eyeing up her tangled mane as a potential nesting spot!

And why . . . ?

One word = pandas.

Today sees world-famous and award-winning Feral Zoo open its gates to two new residents. Giant panda couple Su and Cheng have traveled all the way from China to make Feral Zoo their new home.

Feral Zoo has recently opened the world-class Rare Animal Breeding Center, where Su and Cheng will live. "Feral Zoo is dedicated to the conservation, protection, and care of all animals, but rare animals in particular," said Mr. Feral, owner of the zoo. "We pride ourselves on offering the best care and expertise. Everyone knows that panda numbers in the wild are falling. Here at Feral Zoo it's our duty to nurture and care for Su and Cheng and help them breed."

Mr. Feral owns and runs Feral Zoo with the help of his wife, Mrs. Feral, and three children: Grace, Natty, and Sammy. The three children . . .

Story continues on page 3

Honestly, I haven't seen Mom this worked up since the day a yeti popped in for tea. She's made me polish the zoo gates twice and she's made my younger sister, Natty, scrub all the signposts with a toothbrush. Then she tried to make Grace, my older sister, pick out the weeds in the llama enclosure, but the llamas spat at her and made her cry. Even our dog, Caliban, is scared of Mom today—he's spent the whole day hiding under Dad's desk with his tail between his legs. And all this because we have a couple of pandas arriving. Talk about getting your knickers in a twist!

Don't get me wrong. I love pandas. I love all animals. Especially rare animals. But my specialty is *really* rare animals . . . weird animals. Animals so weird you think they don't exist. Werewolves, yetis, death worms, hell hounds—you name it, I've dealt with it and lived to tell the tale. Yep, that's me.

Sammy Feral = weird animal expert.

So excuse me for not freaking out to the max about two pandas arriving. I mean, it's important—of course it is. But it's not as if the pandas are going to try to eat us when the moon is full. So what's to stress about?

"It's all the journalists, reporters, and TV

crews I'm worried about," Mom snapped at me as I calmly told her to chill out. "I want the zoo to look its best. A panda story is BIG news!"

"Well, let's hope they stick to reporting about the pandas and not some of the other animals we have living here," I said.

"Good point, Sammy. You need to make sure that Donny, Red, and all of their pets stay well away from the main zoo today," Mom warned me. "The reporters aren't allowed to get a whiff of a wish frog, do you understand?"

"Technically the wish frog isn't Donny's and Red's pet," I pointed out. "He just lives with them."

Donny and Red have lived at Feral Zoo ever since my family were turned into werewolves. First they helped me cure them all, and now they help with the other weird stuff that goes on around here. In fact, when it comes to weird, no one knows more than Donny and Red . . .

DONNY

* **Job:** World-famous cryptozoologist (studies animals that supposedly don't exist)
* **Looks like:** A silver fox with gray hair and a cunning gaze
* **Talent:** Knows everything there is to know about weird animals

RED

* **Job:** Cryptozoologist with freaky powers
* **Looks like:** A gothic raccoon
* **Talent:** Powers of telekinesis (she can move things with her mind!)

Most people might think that Donny and
Red are weird. But when
you compare them to
my family—Mom, Dad,
Grace, Natty, and Caliban—
who are all ex-werewolves,
to me they're actually pretty
normal.

ME

* **Job:** Cryptozoologist-in-training
* **Looks like:** A freckly tree frog
* **Talent:** CSC (Cross-Species
  Communication)—I can speak the
  languages of strange animals. Weird,
  right?

Another obvious sign that Mom was in more of
a flap than a crow in a cage was that she let me
have the day off school—so long as I promised
to help out with all the panda preparation, I

could skip out on math and French class. Er, did I need to be asked twice? Of course I stayed at the zoo!

By 6 p.m. this evening the zoo had closed to normal visitors and everyone was getting ready for the Big Arrival.

TV crews and news reporters were stationed outside the zoo's main gate. Large crowds had gathered on the street outside, and there were even a couple of helicopters flying about overhead—all so they could get a picture of the pandas as they arrived.

"Anyone would think the queen was coming for tea," said Natty as we lined up by the gates.

"Pandas are way more important than the queen," I replied.

"Do you think Mom will let me ride one?" Natty asked, wide-eyed and serious.

"I'm pretending you didn't say that, Natty," I said.

"Only joking." She stuck her tongue out at me and laughed.

Honestly, my little sister = half human, half demented monkey child.

"Where are Donny and Red?" Grace asked.

"Backstage," I told her. Backstage is what we call the part of the zoo that's closed off to normal zoo visitors, and it's where Donny and Red live. "They're going to meet us in the Rare Animal Breeding Center when we take the pandas there—once all the TV cameras have gone. I think they're more excited to see the pandas than they were to meet the Mongolian death worm."

Suddenly the hum of noise outside the zoo gates grew louder and louder. People began shouting and cheering, and the flash of camera bulbs lit up the dark evening as the truck carrying our two new pandas pulled up. Thank goodness the truck was soundproofed and had blackout windows. One glimpse outside and the pandas would think they'd arrived at a circus, not a zoo!

Dad pulled open the gates and greeted the waiting crowds with a huge grin.

"This is it!" Natty squealed. "They're finally here!"

As the truck pulled into the zoo, Dad waved his hands at the crowds, gesturing for them to be silent.

"Thank you for coming today. It's amazing to know that we have the support of so many of you as we welcome Su and Cheng to Feral Zoo. Once they are settled we will be inviting members of the public to meet them and see for themselves what wonderful, beautiful creatures giant pandas truly are."

Then Grace, Natty, and I went to stand with Mom and Dad to smile for a few photos with the panda truck. Reporters shouted questions at Dad and camera bulbs flashed around us.

"It's like we're famous!" Grace shrieked as the gates finally closed behind us, shutting out the crowds and TV cameras. "I want to go back and have more pictures taken!"

I rolled my eyes. "Grace, you are lamer than a limping llama. We need to get Su and Cheng into their enclosure, not hang around posing for the cameras."

Grace thumped me on the arm and gave me her best ex-werewolf snarl.

The panda truck drove around to the Rare Animal Breeding Center and made a beeping noise as it backed up toward the pandas' enclosure. Su and Cheng's new home is immense. It has a pond, a small jungle area and a cave for them to sleep in. It's been designed to look and feel just like their natural habitat in China.

"Sorry we missed the circus, kid," said Red, walking up to me. She was wearing her trademark black clothes, black makeup, and bright red hair. "We could hear the crowds shouting all the way from Backstage."

"This is exciting." Donny smiled at me. Let me just make something very clear—Donny NEVER smiles. Not even when we found out the wish frog lived at Feral Zoo. He could ride a unicorn into a river of chocolate and he still wouldn't smile. He's just that kind of a guy. But something about the arrival of the giant pandas was making Donny grin from ear to ear. "Pandas are among the rarest creatures in the world," he said. "Even rarer than a six-eyed sand fairy—and we all know how hard those things are to find!"

Ah, man, Donny knows about all the coolest animals. "So where would you find a six-eyed—"

"Stand back!" Dad shouted, as the truck doors swung open.

Inside was a large crate with two very sleepy-looking pandas surrounded by straw and chewed-up bamboo.

12

One of the pandas stirred and looked out into his new home.

"That's Su," said Max—one of the zookeepers and Grace's boyfriend, "—he's the male." Max helped Dad put a ramp up against the back of the truck.

"We'll get the vet to check that the journey hasn't affected them too much—and then get them settled in their new enclosure," said Dad. "Max, Grace, make sure there's plenty of bamboo and water for them—they're bound to be hungry."

As the vet made her way into the truck

to start checking over the pandas, the rest of us just looked on in awe. Pandas are amazing creatures—so big and gentle and funny-looking. And that's coming from a guy who nearly kissed a yeti once!

The vet moved from Su to Cheng, and just then something caught my eye. A shiny, glistening object nestled among the straw at the back of the truck.

Before I could point it out I felt someone push past me and run up the ramp and into the truck.

"Donny!" I shouted. "I know you're excited to meet the pandas, but we have to wait until the vet—"

"Shh!" Red knocked me in the ribs. "Be quiet!"

I watched as Donny darted to the back of the truck, took off his leather jacket, and used it to swiftly scoop up the object.

He calmly walked back out of the truck, smuggling the strange item under his jacket. His face was as pale as a snow leopard, and any sign of a smile had vanished. He opened his mouth to speak, but all he said was, "Red. Backstage. Now."

Then they walked off without another word.

Not fair!

I was dying to see what Donny had found!

But I'd been waiting to help out with the pandas for weeks. Besides, Mom would roast my guts and eat them with French fries if I went after them— there was way too much to do.

I helped move the pandas into their new enclosure, made sure they had enough fresh bamboo and water, and then I swept out and cleaned the truck they'd traveled in.

"Time to go home for dinner, Sammy," Mom said a couple of hours later.

"Okay, I'll just finish up here and then go and say goodbye to Donny and Red," I said. I couldn't wait to sneak Backstage and see what Donny had found in the pandas' truck.

"Don't be long," Mom warned.

As my family headed off to pick up some fish and chips I quickly finished sweeping up Su and Cheng's enclosure so I could get Backstage. As I swept, the two giant pandas yawned, picked up the bamboo I'd just spent ages shredding and began to chew.

"Hey, this tastes like stale lizard farts."

Er, excuse me?

Am I going crazy, or did I just hear a panda speak?

"What does a guy have to do to get a proper meal around here? Don't you numbskulls know how special pandas are?"

W.H.A.T?

The broom fell from my hands and clattered to the floor.

I spun around, my heart racing, and took a slow step nearer to the pandas.

Su was looking down at the bamboo cane in his

hand in disgust. He threw it on the floor and let out an enormous yawn.

"Did I just hear . . . ?" I muttered. *"Did you just say . . . ?"*

Su looked up at me and blinked in surprise. *"Cheng, I think this kid can understand what we're saying."*

Cheng looked me up and down and nodded with a yawn. *"So maybe you can help us get something decent to eat."*

Oh no. No way. I did not just hear a panda speak. Pandas don't speak—at least, they don't speak to me. I only speak to weird animals. And as rare as they are, pandas are not weird. Not in the slightest. I was imagining things.

Maybe I need to get my ears flushed out? Maybe I have a wax buildup or something gross like that? How else do you explain talking pandas?

I ran out of the Rare Animal Breeding Center toward the Backstage area. The light was on in the kitchen and I walked in to find Donny on one side of the table and Red sitting facing him. Between them sat a large golden egg. After the weird panda conversation, I'd almost forgotten about the strange object Donny had smuggled out of their truck.

I stopped dead in the doorway and rubbed my eyes. First my ears go bonkers and hear pandas talking, and now my eyes were seeing a giant golden egg!

Donny and Red didn't even look up as I walked over to get a better look. It was definitely a golden egg—no trick of the light there. It was covered with small markings that looked like scales.

What kind of animal lays a giant golden egg covered in scales?

I forced down the fear rising inside me.

I knew without asking that whatever I was looking at was bad news.

"We have a problem," Red said, not taking her eyes off the egg.

"An egg-shaped problem?" I said, raising an eyebrow. "What exactly is that thing?"

Donny looked at me seriously. The color had completely drained from his face and his eyes looked sunken into his skull.

"This is no ordinary egg, Sammy." Donny gulped. "It's a dragon egg."

Tuesday, February 24

For most people, the appearance of a golden dragon egg would be a good reason to be late for dinner.

But not for me. And not for my mom.

"I don't care what kind of 'emergency' you're having," Mom had bellowed down the phone at me last night. "You come home for dinner this instant, Sammy Feral, or you'll be sweeping penguin poop with your bare hands for the next month!"

What choice did I have?

"I'll see you guys after school tomorrow," I told Donny and Red. "We can work out what to do with this . . . thing."

I decided not to tell my family about the

dragon egg over dinner last night. Mom worries about me way too much as it is. In my experience, the less parents know about anything weird, the better.

I might get away with lying to my family, but since my best friend Mark got dragged into my weird life, lying to him is out of the question.

MARK

* **Job**: My best friend and an expert in bad jokes
* **Looks like**: A cheeky chimp
* **Interesting fact**: Knows everything weird there is to know about me: my CSC talent, my ex-werewolf family, my crazy friends at the zoo . . . And he STILL wants to hang out. Good friend or what?!

"How did the panda arrival go?" Mark asked when I met him at the school gates this morning. "I'm sorry I couldn't be there. But you know how funny Mom and Dad are about me hanging out at the zoo. No matter how many times I tell them I'm not going to go swimming with the anacondas, they still think it's only a matter of time before I pick up some kind of tropical disease."

"It went pretty well," I said, "but it's what happened when we opened the pandas' truck that's weird . . ." I quickly filled Mark in on the golden dragon egg as we made our way to our first lesson.

"No way!" he gasped. "That's so cool. Why don't dragon eggs just turn up on *my* doorstep?"

"Trust me—be glad this kind of wacko stuff doesn't happen to you. I mean, since when has a dragon egg ever been a good thing? I've never met a dragon, but they're not exactly known for being cute and cuddly."

"So what are you going to do?" Mark asked as we took our seats in class. "Wait until it hatches? Find a way to make it hatch? And who sent it to you? Why? What do you think it has to do with the pandas?"

"All good questions," I whispered, trying to avoid the glare of my teacher as she shouted at the class to be quiet. "I'm heading Backstage after school to figure out some kind of plan with Donny and Red."

"Good idea." Mark nodded. "I'll come too. Mom and Dad are working late."

So after a yawn-inducing day of biology, geography, and history classes, Mark and I headed Backstage (after we'd grabbed a snack at the zoo café of course—at the end of a school day I'm always hungrier than a bear after hibernation!).

Donny and Red were sat around the kitchen table, exactly where I'd left them last night, still staring at the golden egg.

"Ah, Sammy, good afternoon," came a small voice from beside the egg.

"Hi, Wish Frog," I said, finishing off the last of my sandwich. "How are you?"

"I've been better," the wish frog said, frowning. "I was having a perfectly nice day until I discovered that a dragon egg had made its way to Feral Zoo."

WISH FROG

* **Looks like:** An Amazonian horned frog
* **Talent:** Can grant wishes
* **Freaky fact:** Has retired from the wish-granting business and now spends his days chilling out in Feral Zoo's amphibian house.

"I take it this isn't the first dragon egg you've seen?" I asked him.

He shook his little head and hopped toward me. "Let me tell you a thing or two about dragons," he said, nodding wisely. "Dragons were once a very powerful and populous race, but in the last few hundred years their numbers have drastically dwindled."

"Most cryptozoologists believe that dragons are extinct," Donny said, not taking his eyes off the egg. I wondered if he'd done anything but stare at it since it arrived at the zoo.

"That's right," the wish frog agreed. "But a small number of us know that is not the case. Dragons do still exist, but they are incredibly rare."

"So if dragons are dying out," Mark said, walking over to the egg to get a good look at it, "then a dragon egg is pretty precious."

"Worth more than its weight in gold," Red said, nodding.

"So why would someone send it to Feral Zoo?"
I asked.

Donny shook his head. "That's what I just can't
work out. But one thing's for sure . . . this egg has
been fertilized."

Er, rewind!

A fertilized dragon egg = trouble.

"That means it could hatch at any moment!" I
said, panic rising inside me.

"Actually," Donny took a deep breath, "I'd
estimate that we have about a week."

"How can you tell?" Mark asked.

"Markings on dragon eggs are like the rings
in a tree trunk," Red explained. "They show how
old it is and how near it is to hatching. From the
look of these markings, we have no more than
seven days."

"Seven days to figure out exactly what
we're dealing with," Donny said, getting to
his feet and beginning to pace the room, deep

in thought. "We need to know what breed of dragon it is—"

"There's more than one type?" Mark asked.

Red rolled her eyes as if this was the stupidest question in the world.

"The fact that the egg is gold narrows it down to either a Golden Dreq, a Nail Tail or a Fire-Thrower . . ." Donny muttered to himself.

My eyes followed him around the room. "I don't like the sound of a Nail Tail . . ."

"We need to know who sent it here," Donny continued, ignoring me. "And we need to know why. Are we meant to destroy it? Protect it? Whatever the answers are, there's only one way to find out."

"Research," I said confidently. "Books, the Internet, that kind of thing."

Donny shook his head.

"We need more than just research. We need to go back to where this egg came from. We need to go to China."

"China?" I shouted, my mouth falling open like a badger hole. "China the country? On the other side of the world? China with the Great Wall and the Forbidden City and the Terracotta Army? Cool!" I grinned.

A Chinese adventure = awesome!

"When do we leave?"

"We're booked on a flight tomorrow morning," Red replied.

"Tomorrow?" I repeated like a blue-eyed cockatoo. "But I can't go until the weekend, I have school."

"Sorry, kid." Red shrugged. "This can't wait. We need to go quickly, before the egg hatches. And we only have seven days, remember?"

"Red's right." Donny looked at the egg and scratched at his scraggly hair. "With any luck we'll be back here by the weekend with all the answers we need."

"Okay, maybe I'll talk to Mom and Dad," I said, already feeling hopeless.

Letting me miss one day to welcome the pandas was one thing, but skipping school to fly to China in search of dragon danger = no way!

"It's best you stay here, Sammy," Donny said, still staring at the egg. "I need someone to keep an eye on this thing, and my pets need to be fed."

can feed your pets," Mark said helpfully.

"Er, no offense," Red said in a way which made it obvious that she did mean offense, "but we need someone who knows what they're doing when it comes to feeding a gut worm."

My back straightened a little with pride. Sure, Donny's pet gut worm was a cold-blooded killer who'd tried to eat me on more than one occasion, but Red was right, I did know what I was doing.

"I'll be here to keep an eye on the egg," the wish frog reminded Donny.

"It'll take as many of you as possible," Donny said.

So that's settled then.

Donny and Red are flying to China to try to track down the mysterious origins of the golden dragon egg, and Mark and the wish frog and I get to stay at Feral Zoo to keep an eye on the egg and feed Donny's pets. I'm doomed.

Sometimes being a kid sucks worse than a hungry leech.

But then again, there must be something I can do to help the investigation from right here at the zoo. I might not be able to hop on a plane, but I can solve a mystery if I need to.

Sammy Feral = weird-animal detective!

I bet I can find out what breed the dragon egg is! Donny's already said it has to be a Golden

Dreq, a Nail Tail, or a Fire-Thrower . . . How hard can narrowing it down to one be?

I'm going to get to the bottom of this dragon-egg mystery if it kills me.

Although let's hope it doesn't ACTUALLY kill me.

Death by dragon egg is no way to go . . .

Wednesday, February 25
6 days until the dragon egg hatches

Donny and Red left on a 7 a.m. flight to Beijing this morning. I was DYING to start investigating what kind of dragon egg we were dealing with, but first I had to go to school . . . and before school I had to feed Donny's pets . . .

I narrowly escaped a scorching from the phoenix, which burst into flames as soon as I came near it. And the gut worm was as pleasant as ever. *"Sammy Feral, I'd like to eat your guts for breakfast,"* one of his three heads hissed at me, licking his lips with his forked tongue.

The fire-breathing turtle looked a little paler than usual. He didn't even burp a fiery hello at me when I put food in his tank. And I noticed that he hadn't touched his food from the night before. *"Hey, fire-breathing turtle,"* I said in his language. *"Want to tell me what's wrong?"*

"I miss Donny," he said sulkily.

"Well, not eating won't bring him back any faster," I replied. *"Look, I've brought your favorite— dandelion heads!"*

The fire-breathing turtle sighed and pulled his head back into his shell.

A hunger-striking turtle is so NOT what I need right now—I have enough to worry about!

We have less than a week before the dragon egg hatches. Who knows what's going to come crawling out of the shell? But right now it's just sitting on the Backstage kitchen table like a giant chocolate Easter egg waiting to be unwrapped and gobbled up.

"I'll watch the egg while you're at school," the wish frog said. "Do me a favor and leave the window open so some flies can come in. I might get hungry around lunchtime."

"Okay, if you do me a favor and keep an eye on the fire-breathing turtle too," I said. "Try to cheer him up."

Mark was frowning when I met him at the school gate. "I can't come to the zoo this evening.

34

Mom says two nights in a row is out of the question. How am I ever going to become a cryptozoologist if I can't hang out with a dragon egg and a wish frog on a school night?"

Mark's right—his parents really need to cut him some slack.

So after school I made my way to the zoo on my own.

I bumped into Dad as I was walking in. "Remember you have zoo chores to do before you go Backstage, young man."

"Donny's gone away for a few days on business," I told him. "I need to feed his pets."

I also needed to raid Donny's library for books on dragons, but I decided not to mention that one to Dad!

"Well, the pandas need feeding too—make sure they have some fresh bamboo first."

Doh!

The pandas! I'd spent all day worrying about

the dragon egg so I'd nearly forgotten about Su and Cheng. The thought of them brought a grin to my face—I couldn't wait to find out how their first day in the zoo had been.

I found Mom and Max peering into the panda enclosure and taking notes.

"How are they doing?" I asked, dumping my school bag on the floor and pulling my zoo overalls over my uniform.

"Really well," Mom replied. "They seem to have settled in okay, although they're not eating as much as we'd like them to."

"There's fresh bamboo in there," Max pointed at a wheelbarrow out in the yard. "We'll leave you to it."

Max and Mom disappeared into an office to write up their findings for the day, leaving me to shovel out the panda poop, and make sure there was fresh food and water.

Su and Cheng's enclosure is HUGE! It took me

nearly half an hour to track down the two pandas.

"Hey, freckle face," came a voice from behind a small tree.

I turned around thinking I'd see my sister Grace or maybe one of the other zookeepers, but there was no one there. I put a finger in my ear and wiggled it around—I really needed to get that earwax out . . .

I turned back to the poop-strewn floor and started to hum to myself as I swept.

"Hey, freckles!" came the voice again. *"What do we need to do to get a decent meal around here?"*

This time I was not imagining it.

The voice was as clear as a jellyfish.

I slowly turned around. There was no one in the enclosure apart from me, Su, and Cheng.

"I said, what do we have to do to get a decent meal around here?" the voice repeated.

It was coming from Su.

A speaking panda = a clear 8 on the Feral Scale of Weirdness!

"Pandas don't speak," I said, feeling my legs begin to shake beneath me. That's when I realized that not only could I hear them speak, but I could also speak their language.

Wow, pandas really are weirder than a yodeling yeti . . .

"How many pandas have you hung out with before?" Cheng replied. *"You have no idea how special we are."*

Su walked over to me on all fours and spoke again. *"So how about it, freckles?"*

"How about what?"

"How about that food?"

"I've got some fresh bamboo in . . ."

"We don't want boring bamboo!" Cheng objected, padding toward me.

Okay, pandas may look cute and cuddly on TV—but they're still enormous bears. And bears can easily kill people. So I was freaking out like a ferret in a foxhole.

"Please don't hurt me," I said meekly.

"Get us something to eat other than bamboo and we'll consider it."

"Like what?"

"Use your imagination, freckles!" growled Cheng. *"If you'd been in a zoo for two days and not eaten anything but bamboo, what would you want?"*

"I'll tell you what I want," I gulped, trying to feel brave. *"I want to know how I can understand you when you're a . . . you're a . . . you're a panda!"*

"We're not like normal animals," Su replied.

"Well that's obvious," I said. "But why exactly——"

"We're not in the mood for talking!" Cheng shouted at me. "I can't talk or think or do anything when I'm this hungry. Bring me something tasty to eat and we'll tell you whatever you want to know."

"Okay, how about some frozen mice? Or raw steaks? We might have some bird feed by the aviaries if you like?"

"Would you want to eat frozen mice and bird feed?" Cheng shouted again. Boy, that panda was SERIOUSLY grouchy!

"Er, no," I admitted. "But that's the only kind of food we have at the zoo. And the zoo café has closed for the evening . . ."

"So come back tomorrow," Su grunted. "We'll talk then."

Both pandas turned their backs on me and sat down on the floor.

I stood there for a moment, too shocked to know what to do.

"Um, I'll see you tomorrow then," I mumbled, as I backed out of the enclosure.

Great, so not only do I have to worry about feeding Donny's fiery pets and a golden dragon egg that's going to hatch in six days, but I also have to deal with two grouchy, hungry pandas—who can speak!

Can life get any weirder?

I was so busy thinking about the pandas that I walked Backstage in a daze.

"Nothing to report," said the wish frog as I came into the kitchen. "No movement, no color change. If this egg hatches this year I'll be surprised. And the fire-breathing turtle hasn't touched his food all day. I'm worried he's . . . What's wrong with you, Sammy? You look as though you've seen a ghost."

"Not a ghost, just a talking panda." I quickly told the wish frog all about it. "What do you think I should do?" I asked.

"About the talking pandas or getting the fire-breathing turtle to eat?"

"Both," I sighed.

"Maybe you should take the turtle home with you, keep a closer eye on him while Donny's away," the wish frog suggested. "As for the pandas . . . what can you do but feed them and see what they have to say?" He shrugged, not in the least bit surprised that I'd just had a conversation with two pandas. "Who knows—they might even be able to shed some light on the dragon egg. They did come from the same place, after all."

That was a very, very good point.

Man, I'd be lost without the wish frog.

The dragon egg has to be my number-one priority. It's a ticking time bomb—once it hatches, who knows what will happen? I have to find out as much as I can to prepare for whatever lies ahead . . .

I can't ask the pandas about the egg until I have

some food for them tomorrow. But there are more ways to research dragon eggs than to quiz a talking panda!

I took a couple of books on dragons from Donny's bookshelves with me when I left the zoo.

After dinner I went straight up to my room with them, making notes about dragons as I read.

So far, this is what I know . . .

Sammy Feral's Guide
to Dragons

Chapter I:

* A dragon belongs to the reptile family
* A female dragon has a forked tail
* They range from the size of a small dog to the size of a large elephant
* They breathe fire
* There are over 200 subspecies of dragon, each with different characteristics and talents
* They originate from China, but have been known to live all over the world

And this is what I discovered about the three dragon breeds Donny thinks the egg might belong to . . .

GOLDEN DREQ

* Long-extinct breed of dragon
* No one knows what it used to look like

NAIL TAIL

* Has a tail covered in poisonous barbed nails
* Very aggressive
* Uses human bones as toothpicks

FIRE-THROWER

* Has been known to spontaneously combust
* Legend has it that the phoenix evolved from this breed of dragon
* Often found in volcanoes

If the Golden Dreq is long extinct, then the good news is that I've narrowed our egg down to two breeds: a Nail Tail or a Fire-Thrower. The bad news is that when the egg hatches in six days' time, we'll be faced either with a dragon that wants to use our bones as toothpicks or with one that might go up in flames and take the whole zoo with it!

And I still need to figure out why the dragon egg found its way to Feral Zoo.

Hopefully the wish frog's right—maybe the pandas have the answers I need!

Thursday, February 26
5 days until the dragon egg hatches

To: sammy@crypto.com
From: donny@crypto.com

Dear Sammy,

We have arrived safely in Beijing and we're on our way to the panda breeding center that Su and Cheng came from. Hopefully the staff there will have some answers about the pandas' traveling companion!

Nothing else to report here . . .

From

Donny and Red

P.S. I forgot to mention that the phoenix is due to burst into flames any day now.

To: donny@crypto.com
From: sammy@crypto.com

Dear Donny and Red,

Glad you got to China OK. Good luck
with the investigation at your end.

Everything OK here—the phoenix burst
into flames yesterday, so thanks for
the warning! The fire-breathing turtle
hasn't been eating. I'm going to take
him home with me and keep a closer eye
on him.

I've been doing some dragon
investigating of my own. I borrowed
some of your books to read. I hope
that's OK. The egg can't be a Golden
Dreq—they're extinct. I'm not sure
what's worse—a Nail Tail or a Fire-
Thrower! Will e-mail again if there's
any news.

L8ers

Sammy

P.S. The wish frog says hi

I decided not to tell Donny and Red about the
talking pandas. Better that I get some proper

information out of our furry friends before I reveal the shocking truth about them. Besides, I don't want to distract them from the crypto-work they're doing in China.

My first stop after school today was the supermarket (to pick up panda-bribing supplies), and my second stop was the Rare Animal Breeding Center at Feral Zoo.

Su and Cheng were lying down by the pond in their enclosure, yawning and lazily swatting flies away.

"Yo, Max!" I called, seeing him standing just outside the enclosure. "How's it going?"

"Not so great." He frowned. "The pandas haven't eaten anything all day. We're starting to get worried."

"Maybe their bamboo isn't fresh enough?" I suggested, knowing full well that wasn't the problem. "I think Dad had a new delivery today— it's all the way over in the main zoo."

"Great. I'll go and grab some," Max said. "See if they'll eat that instead."

Result! With Max out of the way I was free to go into the panda enclosure and strike up a conversation.

"Don't even think about opening your mouth unless you've brought us something other than stale bamboo," Cheng said grumpily, without even opening her eyes.

"Don't stress it," I said, pulling my backpack off and opening it up. *"I stopped off at the store on my way here and picked up a feast for you."*

Cheng opened one eye and peered out at me suspiciously. Su sat bolt upright, his eyes widening greedily. *"Go on . . ."*

I pulled out the bounty I'd picked up. Cabbages, greens, broccoli, Brussels sprouts, green beans, curly kale . . .

"What in the dragon's name is that?" Cheng said. She didn't sound impressed.

"Just about anything green I could find," I replied proudly. *"And there's enough here to last you at least three days. It's time to start talking, furry. I've got a serious problem I need help with. How do I stop a Nail Tail dragon from using my bones as a toothpick?"*

Su snarled his lip at me. *"You expect us to talk to you, and you bring us cabbage!"*

"Cabbage is a yeti favorite," I said.

"Do I look like a yeti?" Su barked.

Er, is Su seven foot tall, does he stink of cabbage farts and have daggers for claws = no. But I thought it was close enough.

"I'm not eating this garbage," Cheng said, picking up a cucumber and inspecting it with disgust.

"I spent all my pocket money on this. I've got a BIG problem here—a big dragon-egg-shaped problem and you're my only hope! Can't you at least—"

"If someone put a plate of dog barf in front of you, would you eat it just because they had paid money for it?" Su asked angrily.

50

"If anyone was stupid enough to pay money for dog barf, then I'd worry about their—"

"Enough!" Cheng growled. "We have more refined tastes than you, obviously. We want venison burgers with triple-cooked fries, caviar, and chocolate pudding with truffle ice cream. A fine wine from France and maybe some after-dinner mints to finish it all off. Come back tomorrow, and if we're happy, we'll talk. You'd just better hope you don't come face-to-face with a Nail Tail dragon before then . . ."

With that she closed her eyes and lay back on the ground. Su followed suit, ignoring me and the food I'd brought them.

"No wonder you're all dying out," I muttered. *"You're fussier than my sister Natty—and she's an ex-werewolf."*

"Are you still here?" Cheng said, sounding bored.

Honestly, talk about rude! You'd think after days of near starvation a pair of pandas would be a bit more grateful to see some kind of nourishment. How was I ever going to cook them venison burgers and triple-cooked fries without Mom getting suspicious? Everyone knows I'm more useless in a kitchen than a pair of boots on a snake!

Sulking, I went Backstage to feed Donny's pets. I bumped into Dad as I walked past the lion enclosure. "Good day at school, Sammy?"

"Great, until I came to the zoo," I grumbled.

Caliban, our family dog, stood wagging his tail at Dad's side. "Do me a favor and look after Caliban for a bit while I do the zoo rounds?"

"Sure thing, Dad." I smiled. If anything was going to make me feel better about the picky pandas, it was Caliban. Every time he sees me, it's like he thinks I'm the coolest person in the world.

"Come on, boy." I bent down and petted him. "Let's go feed the gut worm."

Caliban continued to wag his tail at my side as I opened the Backstage gate, let us into the yard, and headed for the offices.

There was no sign of the wish frog as I turned on the kitchen light. After a quick look at the egg—which hadn't changed in the slightest, still gold and scaly—I went to feed the pets.

Caliban followed me around the small office building as I dropped a few frozen mice into the gut-worm tank and refreshed the phoenix's water and feed (he's now the size of a small chick and very cute).

The fire-breathing turtle still hadn't touched his food. I'd put fresh dandelions in his tank—his favorite! *"Come on,"* I said to him. *"I'm going to take you home with me tonight so I can keep a closer eye on you. You need to eat something."*

I was back in the kitchen, whistling to myself as I washed up the dirty pet bowls, and thinking about the best way to bake a chocolate pudding for the pandas, when a pigeon landed on the windowsill.

Caliban went CRAZY!

Just the sight of the bird was enough to send him into a tail-wagging frenzy. The pigeon bobbed his head as Caliban growled, wagged, and sprang up toward the window like some kind of demon possessed.

"Oh, Caliban, chill out," I shouted at him. "It's just a pigeon."

Obviously to Caliban it wasn't *just* a pigeon— it was some kind of monster that was about to gobble him up and slaughter everything he loved. The longer the pigeon sat on the windowsill, the more excited and crazed Caliban became. He started to run around the kitchen in circles, then knocked into the table. The dragon egg wobbled from side to side. "Caliban, no!" I shouted. But the sound of my voice only got him more excited. He started running faster, his tail wagging even more manically.

As if in slow motion, I watched as Caliban's back legs sprang up and he leaped onto a chair, from where he vaulted onto the table. His tail spun like a helicopter rotor, knocking the dragon egg up into the air.

I lunged, arms outstretched, watching in slow motion as the dragon egg flew out of my reach and toward the cold hard floor.

I dived for the egg, my arms wide and my hands ready to catch. As my body smacked against the ground, I closed my eyes and braced myself for the sound of the dragon egg smashing. Instead, by an unbelievable stroke of luck, the egg fell into my palms. I quickly clamped my hands around it and pulled it into my chest.

The dragon egg was safe.

For now.

My heart was beating in my throat and blood was gushing around my body like white water rapids. As the pigeon flew off the windowsill, Caliban stopped wagging his tail and tilted his head to one side, looking at me hugging the large golden egg as if I was crazy. Stupid dog!

"Don't worry," I said to the egg. "I'm not letting you out of my sight anymore. I can't risk anything happening to you." My panicked face was reflected in the egg's shiny golden surface. "From now on I'm going to take care of you, I promise."

That's when I made the decision to take the egg home from the zoo and keep it with me at all times.

I walked back from the zoo with the fire-breathing turtle's travel tank under one arm and the golden dragon egg under the other. Most kids my age only have to worry about carrying school books home at the end of the day!

After dinner I spoon-fed the fire-breathing turtle a few mouthfuls of dandelion. He's looking a lot less pale now. One less thing to worry about!

The dragon egg and the fire-breathing turtle's tank are currently next to my bed as I sit up writing in my diary.

This is a nightmare—there's no news from

Donny and I'm no closer to figuring out what to do if the egg hatches.

And we've only got five more days before it does!

Getting the pandas to talk is my only hope. Tomorrow I need to cook the best venison burgers and triple-cooked fries the world has ever seen . . .

Friday, February 27
4 days until the dragon egg hatches

"Hey, Sammy, what's black and white and red all over?" Mark greeted me at the school gates this morning. "A sunburned panda! Get it? Hahahah!"

"Trust me," I said, swinging my heavier-than-usual school bag over my shoulder and walking into the schoolyard. "You would not be joking about pandas if you were unlucky enough to talk to one."

"Huh?" he said.

As we walked to class I quickly told him that not only could I understand Panda, but that Su and

Cheng were two of the grumpiest, pickiest, most miserable mammals I'd ever met.

"So now you need to cook them chocolate pudding with truffle ice cream?" Mark said skeptically as we sat down in class.

"That's not all I have to worry about," I whispered, opening my bag to get out my pencil case and gesturing inside.

Mark's eyes widened with amazement. "Is that what I think it is?"

"I need to keep it safe—" I nodded at the dragon egg "—and I need to keep it secret. No blabbing to any of the other kids at school . . . or the teachers . . . or your parents . . . or *my* parents!"

Mom would KILL me and roast me for dinner if she knew I was carrying a dragon egg around in my schoolbag.

"How many times do I have to tell you, Sammy?" Mark said. "You can trust me."

Mark's right. I can trust him.

Together we took turns looking after the dragon egg at school. We both kept a beady eye on my bag in case the egg started hatching early. And we took turns guarding it on the bag rack outside the dining hall at lunchtime.

Mark even pretended to be sick during PE this afternoon so he could stay with the bag while I ran around the football field.

"No sign of movement," he told me, as I got changed back into my school uniform.

"Good," I said. "Once it hatches, we're in for a rough ride . . . I need to get the pandas onside—they're the only ones that might be able to stop us becoming dragon toothpicks!"

"Well, I've had an idea. My parents aren't home tonight," Mark said. "We can cook up some panda food there!"

So after school Mark and I headed for the supermarket.

Our mission = panda feast.

Why? We need dragon info, fast!

I used what little pocket money I had left and combined it with Mark's. (His parents give him loads of pocket money—and he doesn't even have to sweep out skunk cages to get it. No fair.)

Two hours later we had enough fancy food for two greedy pandas. Hopefully Mark's parents won't mind the fact that we got chocolate on their ceiling, overheated their oven, and smashed four plates and six glasses. I'm way better at zookeeping than I am at cooking! We cleared up as best we could and headed for the zoo.

Cheng and Su were lying facedown in the straw when I opened their enclosure door.

"I think I have something that may just satisfy your needs," I said to them in Panda, feeling smug.

Mark held on to the bag containing the dragon egg as I opened up the picnic basket.

Cheng and Su lazily lifted their heads and eyed me hungrily as I began to pull out the feast Mark and I had prepared.

Two juicy venison burgers with triple-cooked fries on the side, caviar, chocolate pudding with truffle ice cream, and a bottle of French wine we stole from Mark's parents. Fingers crossed they'll be too mad about the mess we made to notice!

I had to admit—it smelled good, and I was STARVING!

Cheng padded over, her nose twitching. Su followed, taking in the banquet in front of them. *"Good effort,"* he whispered, *"but we've already eaten."*

W.H.A.T???

"Excuse me?" I managed to splutter. *"Who else would cook you something like this?"*

"No one," Su admitted. *"But you know as well as everyone else does that pandas only eat bamboo."*

"But you said . . . you said . . ."

"What's going on, Sammy?" Mark asked. "Why aren't they eating?"

"Apparently they won't eat anything but bamboo," I told him, hearing the anger in my voice.

"Can we dig in then?" Mark said, looking down at the food and licking his lips. "I'm starving."

As Mark began to tear into a venison burger, I turned to the pandas. *"Why did you tell me to bring you all this food if you're not going to eat it?"*

"We needed to know how far you would go," Su said. *"We needed to know we could trust you."*

"Trust me with *WHAT?"* I said, utterly confused.

"With what we're about to tell you . . ."

Cheng sat down in the straw and reached for a large stick of bamboo. She began to chew on it thoughtfully. I walked over and carefully took out the golden dragon egg from my schoolbag. *"You know something about this, don't you?"*

"It's a dragon's egg," Su said, stating the obvious. *"About four days away from hatching, by the look of the markings on it."*

"I know all that! But what breed of dragon egg? And who put it in your truck when you left China?" I asked.

"We don't know. We fell asleep as we were leaving the panda center, and when we woke up someone had smuggled it in."

"If you can't tell me who put the egg there, then you can't tell me what I need to know," I said, feeling more annoyed than ever. I sank down to the ground and cradled the egg in my lap. My plan for making the pandas talk had been about as successful as a sloth in a race. The pandas were my only hope—

I had no plan B. Donny's books were worse than useless, and you can't trust anything you read on the Internet. If the pandas couldn't help me then I had to face facts: my bones = toothpicks!

"We share our homeland with dragons. You know that, don't you?" Su said in a whisper. *"As animals we may not look alike, but we have more in common than you know. Dragons and pandas are both very, very special creatures . . ."*

My ears pricked up, and I tried to block out the sound of Mark slurping down truffle ice cream as I listened to Su.

"Long ago, the great plains of China were filled with pandas and dragons."

Maybe the pandas did know something about dragons after all!

"There was once a flourishing community of dragons throughout the whole of Asia. They roamed the forests, swam in the lakes, soared through the skies. Large dragons, small dragons, golden dragons, green dragons,

friendly dragons, beastly dragons—all of them were free to live their lives."

"*What happened?*" I asked.

"*You know more about strange animals than most people, freckles,*" Cheng said. "*Dragons aren't ordinary creatures. They have powers—magical powers.*"

"*Like what?*"

"*Depends on the breed,*" Su said. "*Some dragons have scales that can turn invisible. The blood of others can be used to cure any illness. Some have wings that can take you to the depths of the ocean, as well as high in the sky. And others can turn objects to gold with their fiery breath.*"

Wow.

"*I think this egg is either a Nail Tail or a Fire-Thrower,*" I said quickly. "*What can you tell me about them? When it hatches I need to know how I can protect everyone—how can I fight it?*"

"*A dragon is not to be fought,*" Su said gravely. "*No matter how dangerous it is—a dragon should be protected. Since man first discovered a dragon, they have* been hunted for their magical properties. Their blood has been used in potions, their skin worn as cloaks. Mankind has hunted dragons almost out of existence. What was once a very proud and strong species is now nothing but an echo of their former selves."

"There are only a few dragons left," Cheng added, "and they live in the last dragon refuge in the world."

"Where's that?" I asked.

"The Dragon Temple."

"The Dragon Temple?" I repeated in a whisper. "Where's that?"

"It's their last stronghold. Their sole remaining sanctuary. But its location is a secret. There are some among us who will tell you that the Dragon Temple doesn't even exist. That it's nothing more than a legend."

I sprang to my feet, carefully putting the dragon egg back into my bag. "Mark, we need to go," I said quickly. "I have to e-mail Donny right away—he needs to find the Dragon Temple."

"What about Donny's pets?" Mark said, licking

the last few chocolate-pudding crumbs from his fingers. "Someone needs to feed them today."

"Okay, you do that," I said. Mark smiled at me proudly, obviously pleased that I trusted him with the task. "I'll go and e-mail Donny."

"*Your friend won't find the Dragon Temple,*" Su said, as I was about to walk away. "*Not if the Dragon Temple doesn't want to be found.*"

"*What choice do we have?*" I asked. "*If I can't fight a dragon that might turn me to ash, then I need to know what else I can do to protect myself . . .*"

"*A dragon egg won't hatch unless it's bathed in fire,*" Cheng told me with a yawn.

"*Fire?*"

"*Once the egg is ripe——*" the panda pointed to the markings on the egg "*——the dragon mother will bathe it in fire and it will hatch.*"

"*So without fire, it won't hatch?*" I said, my voice filled with hope. "*Even if it's ready to?*"

Cheng shook her head. Phew!

69

Sammy Feral = 1, dragon egg = 0.

I e-mailed Donny as soon as I got home.

To: donny@crypto.com
From: sammy@crypto.com

Donny,

You need to find the Dragon Temple.
Don't worry, we have a bit more time
than we thought we did—the egg won't
hatch unless it's bathed in fire. And I
don't intend to go bathing the egg in
fire any time soon . . . How dumb would
that be?

Sammy

Donny e-mailed me back right away.

To: sammy@crypto.com
From: donny@crypto.com

Sammy,

There's no such place as the Dragon
Temple. It's a myth. How's the fire-
breathing turtle doing?

Donny

```
To: donny@crypto.com
From: sammy@crypto.com

Donny,

Fire-breathing turtle is fine—he's been
staying with me. Temple not a legend.
It exists.

Sammy
```

Donny hasn't e-mailed me back yet.

The dragon egg is resting on my pillow as I write this.

The fire-breathing turtle is looking better. He ate a whole dandelion head this evening. I think he'll be well enough to go back to the zoo tomorrow.

Tomorrow is Saturday. Maybe I can hop on a flight to China and go and find the Dragon Temple myself?

Saturday, February 28

Tap. Tap. Tap.

It was early morning. Way too early to get up. Too early for my alarm clock to go off. Too early for the sun to be peeping through the curtains. Too early for Mom to be screaming at me to get out of bed and get to the zoo for a day's work.

Tap. Tap. Tap.

It sounded like rattling. Like someone tapping at the window.

I threw off the duvet and rubbed my eyes as I walked over to check it out.

There was nothing there.

Tap. Tap. Tap.

Then I realized the noise was coming from behind me—from my bed.

Tap. Tap. Tap.

It was getting louder.

Suddenly a ball of flame lit up my room like a firework. The fire-breathing turtle was wide awake and burping fire all over the egg! The tapping sound grew into a rattling, and the rattling grew into a cracking.

I whirled around and dived for my bedside lamp. I turned it on and stood back in horror as the golden dragon egg on my pillow shook from side to side.

Once again the fire-breathing turtle burped a large cloud of fiery ash all over it. A large crack appeared down its center. It was hatching!

What was I thinking? Leaving a dragon egg next to a fire-breathing turtle? How could I be so STUPID?

The egg was hatching and it was all my fault. In no time at all I'd have a killer dragon on my hands . . .

The crack split the egg in two, and before I knew it two small bat-like wings were nudging through the top of the shattered eggshell.

My mouth hung open and I gulped down my fear as I watched the baby dragon emerge.

First its head poked out. Two tiny golden eyes looked around the room nervously. The remaining shell dropped away and the newborn dragon clumsily fell onto my bed, face-first into the mattress.

I quickly looked at its tail—no big nail-like barbs. Phew—it wasn't a Nail Tail dragon. It had to be a Fire-Thrower . . .

Yikes!

That meant it could spontaneously combust at any moment!

Beginning to panic, I looked around the room for anything I could use to put out the flames the dragon was surely going to throw my way. I reached for a glass of water on my bedside table . . .

I stood as still as a statue, watching as the dragon managed to pull itself onto its hind legs and lift its head up. It peered around my room, taking in the world for the first time. The dragon's eyes fixed on me and it let out a little fiery burp. *"Mommy?"* it said.

WHAT?!

"Er, no, there's been a mistake," I replied in Dragon. *"I'm not your—"*

"Mommy!" the dragon cried out, flapping its wings and rising from my bed.

Its wings flapped once, twice, and then the dragon nose-dived toward the floor and landed on my bedroom carpet with a loud THUD.

Ow—that had to hurt!

The newborn dragon sat up, its golden eyes spinning in its head. *"I don't know flying . . . Mommy teach me?"* Once again the dragon began to flap its wings and it rose off the ground in clumsy circles.

I ducked away from it, landing back on my bed and pulling the duvet over my head, the glass of water—my only protection—still in my hand. I stupidly thought that if I hid from

the dragon maybe it wouldn't think I was its mother.

"Mommy!" it shrieked again.

The next thing I knew there was a loud burping noise and then the duvet above me burst into flames.

Argh!!

I quickly threw the glass of water onto the fire. It sizzled out, leaving a charred black hole in the fabric.

"No, bad dragon!" I said sternly to the small creature, now crouched at my feet and licking my toes. It was as big as a large rat and its body was covered with shimmering golden scales.

It looked up at me and widened its golden eyes. *"No fire?"*

"No fire," I agreed. *"Fire bad."*

"Fire bad?" It looked confused.

The tiny dragon spread its wings, reminding me of a flying dinosaur, and lifted itself from the duvet. With a few clumsy movements it hovered up to me so it looked me right in the eye. *"Mommy?"* it said again.

I had a split second to decide what to do . . .

"Yes," I said. *"I'm your mommy—your father—your parent. And you must do as I tell you to. Understand?"*

The tiny dragon nodded.

"And no fire inside the house. Fire bad."

The dragon flapped its wings and began to swoop around the room, knocking into my bookshelves. It swept my crocodile-tooth collection clean off the shelf. My framed animal-first-aid certificate fell to the ground and smashed. The dragon let out a loud *"Cawwww!"* and carried on, destroying everything it touched.

"No!" I said as quietly as I could, following the dragon around and trying to pick up the crocodile teeth and pieces of smashed picture frame from the ground. *"No flying!"*

I heard the sound of footsteps on the landing.

Great—the dragon had woken someone up!

Mom and Dad had no idea I'd been keeping the fire-breathing turtle in my room the last few days—let alone a dragon egg.

I'd be grounded until I had gray hair if they ever found out!

"*Shhhh,*" I said to the dragon. "*Sleep time. Be quiet now.*"

"*Me not tired,*" it replied. "*Me hungry!*"

"*Okay, I'll get you some food. Just please——*"

"Arghhhhhh!!!!!" The sound of Natty's scream nearly pierced my eardrums. I clapped my hands over my ears as I turned around and saw both of my sisters—Grace and Natty—standing in my bedroom doorway.

Grace clamped her hand over Natty's mouth, pulled her into the room and quickly shut my door behind them.

"Sammy, *what* is going on?" she said in her best angry-big-sister voice.

The dragon landed on my shoulder. "*No fire,*" it said in my ear.

"*No fire,*" I repeated. "*Especially not in front of Auntie Grace and Auntie Natty.*"

"Ooh av a et aagon?" Natty mumbled. Grace slowly took her hand away from Natty's mouth. "You have a pet dragon?" she said, her eyes wide with shock.

"Not exactly . . ." I began to explain.

"Mom's going to ground you for all eternity when she finds out," Grace said smugly, crossing her arms.

"She can't find out. You have to help me, Grace. Please," I begged. "I'll owe you, big time. I'll do anything you want. Anything. I promise. Just help me, please."

"You'll owe me too," Natty said, walking over to my bed and inspecting the large burned-out hole in my duvet and the shattered pieces of dragon eggshell on my pillow.

"I'll owe you both."

"Okay," Grace agreed. I could tell by the look on her face that she was already cooking up some kind of evil plan to make me pay her

81

back. At that moment I would have agreed to anything—I'd even shave her back hair at the next full moon if she helped me keep the dragon a secret.

"We need to get him to the zoo," Grace said firmly. "Donny will know what to do with him."

"Donny's not technically *at* the zoo at the moment," I said, "but I'll e-mail him right away and tell him to come back."

I stood there in my pajamas as she reeled off commands. "Natty, go and get Caliban's leash from the kitchen. And some food from the fridge and a water bowl. Sammy, you need to explain to the dragon that we're taking it to its new home and it needs to behave."

I think this was the first and only time in my life I've actually been grateful for Grace's bossiness.

Under the cover of darkness, as the sun rose in the early morning sky, Grace, Natty, and I walked to the zoo in our pajamas, with my new pet dragon flying on a dog leash behind us.

A definite 9 on the Feral Scale of Weirdness.

As soon as I arrived Backstage I wrote Donny
an e-mail.

To: donny@crypto.com
From: sammy@crypto.com

Donny,

Dragon has hatched! It's a Fire-
Thrower! Come back NOW!

Sammy

Sunday, March 1

The last twenty-four hours = pure STRESS!

In my pre-weird life (before my family became werewolves, before I met Donny and Red, and before I ever knew that weird animals existed) I used to think that it would be cool to have a baby dragon as a pet. But how wrong was I?

Dragons, especially baby dragons, are HARD WORK.

I haven't even had a chance to sit down and write in my diary—it's been so crazy.

I don't know that much about Fire-Thrower dragons, but the fact that they can throw fire means we're in for some trouble! I've spent today trying to flameproof Backstage . . .

* I've put bottles and glasses of water on every surface
* I've thrown out anything flammable
* I'm following the dragon around with a fire extinguisher at all times

So far there's been no sign of any fire-throwing. But where does a dragon throw fire from? Its nostrils? Its mouth? Who knows—it could have super-flame-throwing farts! I'm taking no chances. There's no peeing, pooping, or farting allowed inside, just in case!

"No, if you want to pee you have to go outside," I told the dragon for the billionth time this morning.

"No pee-pee inside?" the dragon replied.

"No, absolutely not," I repeated in Dragon, ushering the tiny thing into the Backstage yard. "Good dragon," I said in English.

"His name is George," Natty said, all matter-of-fact. Both my sisters were sitting on a bench talking to the wish frog.

"The wish frog has just been telling us the best way to bathe George," Grace informed me.

"Er, rewind," I said. "Since when has the dragon's name been George?"

"I named him," Natty said simply. "George, no!" she shouted, springing out of her seat and running toward the small dragon, who was hovering by one of the old werewolf cages out in the yard. "You need to pee over by the bushes."

George cocked his head to one side and stared at my little sister in confusion.

"He doesn't understand English," I told Natty, before repeating the instruction again in Dragon. "And who said you got to name him?" I asked, feeling annoyed. George hatched in MY room. He thinks I'm his mother. I should be the one to name him!

"You owe us for helping you, Sammy," Natty replied, crossing her arms. "I spent all of yesterday feeding him and putting out fires, and I haven't said one word to Mom or Dad. The least you can do is let me name him."

I hate it when my sisters are right. Natty had helped me way more than I'd expected since the dragon was born. I did owe her. But I thought that would just involve letting her dress me up as a human hamster and trying to make me do tricks—not naming the dragon!

"Why George?" I asked.

"I named him after George and the dragon," she replied. "Come on, George, back inside now." Natty took hold of the dragon's leash and began to pull him back toward the offices.

"George was the knight who *killed* the dragon," I pointed out. "And dragons don't speak English!"

"His name is George!" she said impatiently.

"And if he's going to live here at Feral Zoo, then he needs to learn English!"

"Don't you think we should keep him out here in the yard instead of inside?" Grace said. "He's kind of a fire hazard after all. Maybe we could adapt one of the old werewolf cages for him?"

"There's no point in keeping a dragon in a cage," the wish frog said wisely. "One fiery breath could burn through the bars if he wanted to. Besides, keeping George in a cage would be cruel."

"I agree," I said. "I wish we could keep him outside, but we can't risk him flying up into the air for all the zoo visitors to see. We have a hard enough time keeping all the Feral Zoo weirdness a secret, without a dragon soaring through the skies above us."

"We'll just have to train him not to fly too high." Grace shrugged, as if training a dragon was as easy as teaching a fish to swim.

"Given that I can't even get him to pee outside without incinerating everything in his path, I think restricting his flight movements will be tricky!"

"I'll train him," Grace offered.

Er, excuse me, what?

There had to be some kind of hidden catch. Grace never helps me out with stuff. She's normally moodier than a hippo with a headache.

"I'll train him," Grace said again. "I'm the best animal trainer here at Feral Zoo."

That much was true. Grace has trained everything from a chimp to a chipmunk.

"What do you want in return?" I said suspiciously.

"A favor," she said slowly.

"I already owe you one favor, Grace," I pointed out. "For not telling mom when George hatched."

"Okay, so owe me a big favor."

"I'm not shaving your back hair at the next full moon, Grace, forget it!"

Grace's face turned red and I looked for signs of steam coming out of her ears. "I do *not* have back hair," she said through gritted teeth.

Yeah, right!

"I want you to help Max out with his new project. If you do that, then we're even."

As well as being a zookeeper, Grace's boyfriend, Max, is studying at the Royal College of Zoology. The last time I helped him out involved letting him study a rare Mongolian death worm. Max might be soppier than a bucket of bubble bath (I once accidentally read a love letter he'd written to Grace and nearly puked my guts out), but he's okay. If all Grace wanted me to do was help Max out, then I was definitely getting off easy. Way better than shaving back hair!

"Done." I stuck out my hand and Grace shook it. "You train George to live outside without scaring away the zoo visitors, and I'll help Max in any way I can."

"Great, I'll start today . . ." Grace began to walk toward the offices, where Natty had taken George.

"Wait." I stopped her. "Just give me a few minutes alone with George. I need to speak to him about something."

Natty was trying to brush George's scales with a dog-grooming brush when I came into the kitchen. Poor George was flinching away from her, but she was holding him on a short leash.

"Natty, I need a few minutes alone with George."

"Okay. Bye-bye, Georgie." She blew him a sloppy kiss. "I'll be back for your bath in a minute."

"Sorry about that," I said to George in Dragon.

"Girl poked me with stick," he said, looking glum.

"It's called a hairbrush, and don't worry, I won't let her do it again."

"Mommy, me be good," he said, looking up at me with his small golden eyes. *"Me did not burn fire on small girl and me did pee-pee outside."*

"Yes, very good boy, George." I patted his scaly head. *"You must always pee-pee outside and absolutely do not, under any circumstances, set fire to my sister—or to anyone else for that matter. Oh, and before I forget—my other sister, your Auntie Grace, is going to help teach you how to live outside."*

"Okay, Mommy."

"But before she tries to train you, I need to ask you about where you came from."

"*I came from egg, Mommy.*"

"*Before that. Do you know anything about the Dragon Temple or anything about other dragons at all?*"

I was pretty sure asking him was useless—but it was worth a shot.

"*You a dragon, Mommy?*" he asked, looking confused.

"*No,*" I stroked his wing and he waddled into my lap. "*I'm not a dragon. But I'm going to look after you, don't worry. I'm going to find out who you really are and why you're here.*"

"*Me here so you can love me.*" He looked up and blinked innocently at me.

I smiled down at him.

Oh man, this is not good, not good at all.

I'm getting attached to a dragon, and he's already attached to me!

George isn't a dog or a hamster. He's not cute and cuddly. He can't sleep at the end of my bed and keep me company on long walks. He's a fire-breathing beast who doesn't belong here.

I need to find out who he is and where he belongs before it's too hard to say goodbye!

Monday, March 2

To: sammy@crypto.com
From: donny@crypto.com

Sammy,

Is everything OK? How is the dragon?
My calculations about the markings
on the egg must have been wrong—I
should have known it was due to hatch
earlier.

Has anyone suspicious come to the zoo?

We are trying our hardest to get home,
but our flight has been delayed. Be
back with you tomorrow, I hope.

Call me if there's an emergency.

Donny

To: donny@crypto.com
From: sammy@crypto.com

Donny,

All OK here. It was a bit of a shock to us that the egg hatched a few days early! The dragon's name is George, and Grace is trying to train him to live outside without flying so high that people can see him.

See you tomorrow.

Sammy

It's a bit of a bummer that Donny and Red are delayed getting back from China. Don't get me wrong—I have everything under control here. The pets are fed and George is as cute as can be—but today is Monday and that can only mean one thing.

School.

"You can't take a day off school, Sammy," Mom said sternly when I asked her on the phone. Grace and I spent last night Backstage at the zoo—but

Mom made Natty go and sleep at home. "You had a day off last week when the pandas arrived."

"But I'm sick!" I protested.

"No, you're not," Mom argued. "You've spent the weekend looking after Donny's pets, and you haven't done any of your zoo chores. You're in hot water already, young man, so don't try to pretend you're unwell to get a day off school!"

"What am I going to do?" I said to Grace as I put down the phone.

"Well, you can't leave him here," Grace said, looking over at George, who was sleeping in Caliban's old dog bed. "Without his mommy he'll burn the place down."

She had a point.

George was doing well with his training, but no way was he ready to be left for an entire day.

I had no choice.

I'd have to take him to school.

"I need you to get in the bag and be as still and quiet

98

as possible," I said to George, after I'd woken him up and fed him some cucumber for breakfast. *"Pretend you're asleep."*

"Me sleep here?" George said, peering into my empty school bag. *"In a cave?"*

"Absolutely! You need to sleep in this cave, a cave that I'm going to carry around on my back all day."

"Oh, me go on Mommy's back to fly!" George said with delight, waddling toward the bag.

"Something like that," I mumbled. *"Tell me if you need a pee-pee. Don't pee in here, okay?"*

"Okay, Mommy."

So I set off for school with a dragon in my backpack.

A scary 7 on the Feral Scale of Weirdness.

"Hey, Sammy, why do pandas have fur coats?" Mark grinned at me as I met him at the school gates. "Because they'd look stupid in leather jackets!"

"I'm really not in the mood for panda jokes today," I said. We walked to our classroom and took our seats. "In fact, I hope today flies by as quickly as a speeding peregrine falcon."

"Dragon-egg trouble?" Mark asked. "How many days left on the countdown until it hatches?"

I leaned over to whisper in Mark's ear. "The dragon is no longer an egg. That's the trouble."

"Quiet down, please, class!" our teacher shouted at us. "And, Sammy Feral, if I catch you talking to Mark again during class, I'll have no choice but to make you move seats."

I opened my math textbook and tried not to look

at Mark. I knew he'd be desperate to find out what had happened after the egg hatched. He'd fly off his chair and splatter all over the ceiling if he knew I was carrying the tiny dragon around in my backpack.

"Psst, Sammy," Mark whispered, as the teacher turned and began to write out a math equation on the whiteboard. I ignored him. The last thing I needed was the teacher to give me a blasting—I had to avoid that kind of attention while I was carrying a dragon around.

"Sammy!" Mark said again, a little louder.

Toby in the row in front of us looked around, his nose twitching. "Anyone else smell burning?"

Oh no . . .

Katrina turned around and stared right at me.

"Sammy, your bag . . ." Mark hissed.

I looked down. What the . . . uh-oh . . . bad news!

Smoke was coming from the bag and a small hole had been burned into the side of it.

Panic time!

I shot up from my seat, grabbed the bag, and ran for the classroom door. "Sammy, where do you think you're going?" the teacher asked sternly.

"I need the bathroom . . ."

"You'll have to wait." She pointed to my empty chair. "Sit back down."

I quickly put my bag behind my back, aware that smoke was billowing out of it and wafting all around me. "Please, miss," I pleaded. My brain scrambled to think up an excuse. But how do you explain a trail of smoke? All I could do was sacrifice my street cred once and for all . . .

"It's my butt. I have a case of explosive diarrhea. Mom cooked her famous Bombay curry last night and just a fart alone can make my pants smoke."

Everyone in the class burst out laughing.

The teacher looked at me in horror, but before I could say anything else I felt heat lick at my back. I turned around, opened the classroom door, and ran.

I bolted for the boys' bathroom across the hall and closed the door behind me. I quickly took off my smoldering school blazer and dumped it in a sink, turning the cold tap on and quenching the small fire that was beginning to take hold.

Suddenly a cannonball of flames erupted from my feet and I looked down to see George flapping his wings and looking up at me apologetically. *"Sorry, Mommy. Me did fire. Me bad dragon."*

I desperately stamped at the floor and tried to splash water from the sink onto the growing flames. The bathroom door flew open. My heart nearly stopped in my chest and I looked up expecting a teacher to catch me red-handed with a dragon. But it was Mark.

"Whoa!" he said, looking down at George in awe. "Can he fly?"

"Yes, he can fly—and if you hadn't noticed, he also breathes fire!"

"Oh, right," Mark edged past George and began to stamp at the blazing schoolbag. In a matter of seconds we'd managed to extinguish it completely. "Thank goodness we didn't set off the fire alarm."

I looked up at the fire alarm half hanging off the ceiling. "I'm pretty sure it's illegal to not have working fire alarms in a school."

"The ones over by the science block work," Mark said. "Tommy set them off last term by setting fire to his farts—remember?"

I did remember, but laughing about fart jokes was not an option for me at that moment. "Mark—George. *George—Mark*," I introduced them.

Mark bent down and shook George's wing, "How do you do? I've never met a dragon before."

"No fire at boy?" George looked up at me.

"No, George, no fire at anyone. I need to take you home. You can't be here with me."

"I stay with you, Mommy." George nodded.

"No, you can't stay with me."

"But I good now, I promise."

"You are good, George. It's not your fault you set my

105

bag on fire—you're a dragon; you can't help breathing fire. You can't control it yet. But this is no place for you. I need to get you back to the zoo."

George let out a whining sound and began to cry. Golden snot began to pour from his nose and small puffs of fire spluttered onto the bathroom tiles as he began to sob. *"I stay with you, Mommy. Me no go home."*

"Yes, George, you need to go . . ."

He began to wail louder and louder.

"Shhhh!" I said desperately. *"People will hear you."*

"Arghhh!" he sobbed. *"I is naughty and Mommy not want me!"*

"No, I do want you. Just, please, be quiet!"

His wails got more piercing and his fiery breath blew out in huge fireballs—Mark had to leap out of the way to avoid a blazing. *"Okay, okay, be quiet. You can stay,"* I said hastily. *"If I let you stay with me, you have to promise to be quiet. And not to burn anything unless I tell you to. Okay?"*

"*Yes, Mommy, I promise.*" George sniffed away his tears and smiled up at me.

"Right," I said to Mark. "You have to help me keep a dragon at school today. And we need to keep him hidden . . ."

The rest of the day passed in a busy blur as Mark and I did everything we could to keep George a secret.

* I smuggled George into English underneath Mark's blazer and he happily slept behind a pile of books

* I took him into chemistry and he was very handy to have there when my Bunsen burner failed

✱ I sat outside in the rain and ate lunch with him while everyone else was in the dining hall

✱ I hid him inside a papier-mâché model of a volcano in the geography classroom—no one batted an eyelid when the volcano top started smoking!

"The school day's nearly over, Sammy," Mark reassured me. "Just one more period to go."

"I don't think George will survive another class," I said honestly. "I don't want to push our luck. I need to get him to the zoo as soon as possible. I have an idea. It involves the fire alarms at the science block."

Mark smiled at me, reading my mind.

As the bell for the next period began to ring we both made our way toward the science block. George was under my arm, wrapped up in my smelly old gym shorts. When we came to the corridor with the fire alarm Tommy had set off last term, I lifted my smelly gym shorts with George inside them up toward the alarm. *"George,"* I whispered.

"Yes, *Mommy,*" came his little voice from inside the bundle.

"On the count of three, I need you to let out a big fiery breath."

"Me not allowed fire inside anymore," he replied.

"On this one occasion you are. Ready? One, two . . ."

A huge fireball erupted from my gym shorts and in a matter of seconds the fire alarm was blaring out through the school.

The school corridor erupted into chaos. Everyone was running for their fire-drill stations, teachers were screaming for people not to run, and every alarm in the school had started to sound.

"Now's our chance to get away!" I shouted to Mark.

We ran out of the school gates and all the way to the zoo without looking back.

Dodging the other zookeepers so they wouldn't report us to Mom and Dad for skipping school, we managed to reach Backstage. Mark and I collapsed in a heap on the ground as soon as we were behind the safety of the Backstage gate.

George hopped out from under my arm and shook off what was left of my charred gym shorts.

"Mommy did fly and she did carry me," he said with a smile. *"Fun!"*

"I don't think I've ever run so fast," I panted.

"I had trouble keeping up," Mark admitted, gasping for breath. "What with you running for your life and that boy chasing after us . . ."

"What boy?" I said quickly.

"That boy . . . You didn't see him?"

I shook my head.

"He was wearing a kung-fu outfit with a black belt around it. I think we managed to lose him as we came into the zoo—he needed to line up for a ticket to get in."

I looked over at George, my heart beating harder now. Someone was following us.

This was not good news at all!

Tuesday, March 3

Thank the bearded dragon, Donny and Red are BACK from China! Their plane landed early this morning and they came straight to the zoo.

"I thought your e-mail said its name was George?" Donny was looking at the dragon curiously, scratching his head of gray hair.

"Natty named him," I said.

"And I thought you said you'd read a few of my dragon books?" Donny raised an eyebrow.

"I did. So?"

"So you should know," he said, "that a dragon with a forked tail, like this one—" he pointed to the forked end of George's golden tail "—is a female."

A female!

"George is a girl?" I spluttered, feeling stupid. Now that I think about it, I do remember reading that somewhere . . .

"Georgina," Red smiled, bending down to pat the tiny dragon on the head. Georgina smiled up at her and let out a sizzling sigh.

"Thanks for looking after my pets," Donny said, peering into the tank of the fire-breathing turtle, who was now living back at the zoo.

"Well, you're on feeding duty today. I need to get to school. There's no way I'm taking Georgina with me again so you'll have to dragon-sit too."

"My pleasure." Donny grinned. "I've always wanted to study a dragon. I'm sure Georgina and I will get on like a house on fire."

"Be careful what you wish for . . ." I warned him. I slung a plastic bag containing my school books over my shoulder (must remember to buy another bag!) and headed for the door.

"Oh, I nearly forgot." I turned back to Donny. "Pandas are weird animals too."

"Say what?" Red said.

"I can speak to them—they're as weird as waltzing wallabies. See you after school—bye!"

"Sammy, wait . . ."

I was out of the door and on my way to school before I could get caught up in another conversation with Donny. To tell you the truth, I was glad to be leaving Backstage for the day. Sometimes things really can get a bit too weird, even for me. For once it might be nice to have a normal day at school.

"Hey, Sammy, why do dragons sleep during the day? So they can fight knights!"

"Hey, Mark," I said, rolling my eyes.

"Did you bring George with you today?"

I shook my head. "Donny and Red are back and babysitting, thank goodness. Oh, and George is a she, not a he. Her name's Georgina."

That was about as near to normal as my conversations got today. About five minutes later my phone buzzed in my pocket. It was a text from Donny:

Come bk to zoo NOW! G going crazy without u here!

I waited until break to text him back.

I can't skip skl again.

He texted back right away.

She's setting fire to things. Flapping about. Whimpering . . .

I'll be there straight after skl. Promise.

So much for my normal day!

And what happened to me on the way to the zoo = a freaky 5 on the Feral Scale of Weirdness . . .

Every step of my journey, I couldn't shake the feeling that someone was watching me. But every time I turned around to look, there was no one there.

As I walked through the park, around the duck pond, past the shops, and all the way to the zoo, I kept looking over my shoulder, convinced that someone was following me.

Maybe I was imagining it?

Maybe the dragon dramas of the last few days were making me insane?

But just as I reached the zoo I turned a corner and saw him—the flash of a kung-fu outfit, a black belt tied around the waist.

There *was* a boy following me! But as soon as I spotted him he was swept up into a crowd of zoo visitors and disappeared from sight. I tried to find him—I moved quickly through the crowd and searched everywhere—but he'd vanished into thin air.

I wasn't imagining it, and I'm not crazy. I'm being followed.

And the boy following me looks about as friendly as a black mamba with a toothache!

Who is he, and what does he want with me?

Wednesday, March 4

I made another quick stop-off at the zoo before school this morning. I'd arranged to meet Mark Backstage—he had a secret weapon to help Georgina. But first I dropped in to see the pandas. I had a few questions for them . . .

"You must have some idea who this boy is?" I said to Cheng in Panda.

"Why would we know anything about some karate kid following you about?" Cheng replied with a shrug, sucking on a piece of bamboo.

"Isn't it a little bit coincidental that just after both of you arrive from China with a dragon egg to

keep you company, a boy dressed as a kung-fu expert starts following me about?"

"You're probably just being paranoid," Su sighed wearily. "It must be the lack of sleep that's making you loopy— it happens to all new parents."

"Oh, so you heard about the dragon egg hatching then?" I asked.

"And the fact that the dragon thinks you're its mom— yes, we've heard all about it from the wish frog. No thanks to you, of course. You haven't been to visit us in days."

"I've been kind of busy," I said defensively. "I'm sorry if you think I've abandoned you, but—"

"Don't sweat it, freckles," Cheng said, spitting her chewed-up bamboo dregs on the ground. "We have everything we need right here. Fresh food and water, shelter, plenty of space. We've never been happier. The last thing we need is you hanging around all the time and trying to talk to us about dragons and Dragon Temple Guardians."

Er, excuse me, what?

"*Dragon Temple Guardians?*" I raised an eyebrow. "*I didn't say anything about that.*"

"*You said a boy in kung-fu gear has been following you around.*" Su shrugged and carefully selected another piece of bamboo. "*You know, Sammy, all you ever do is ask us about dragon stuff . . . don't you want to know about us? Pandas are very special animals . . . more special than you know . . .*"

"*I'm sure pandas are as special as a sparkling starfish in a spacesuit, but right now I need to know who is following me around . . .*"

"*Maybe if you came by and spent a bit more time with us, we could tell you more . . .*" Su raised her eyebrows.

"*Spend more time with you?*"

"*Entertain us.*" Cheng grinned mischievously. "*Sing us some songs, dance about in a clown hat—that kind of thing.*"

"*No way.*" I shook my head. "*I see what you're trying to do. I've jumped through enough hoops for you guys* already. *Either tell me the truth or I'm out of here."*

"Just one song." Cheng fluttered her eyelashes. *"Please?"*

I looked down at my watch. I was running late for school.

"I don't have time for this." I shook my head. *"I'll see you later."*

Cheng and Su nodded to each other as I left their enclosure, shutting the door behind me.

Honestly, am I some kind of funny game to the pandas? Oh, let's make Sammy cook us a fancy meal, let's get him to sing us songs and dance around in a stupid hat!

No way!

I am not being fooled by them again! I'll find some way to make them tell me what they know about Dragon Temple Guardians—and it won't involve wearing a clown hat!

I don't need three guesses to figure out why a Guardian might be following me.

He wants to kill me.

He thinks I've stolen a precious dragon egg and now made the dragon think I'm its mother. And now the Dragon Temple Guardians want to punish me by making me die a slow and painful death.

Brilliant! NOT!

I've fought some fearsome creatures in my time, but I don't like my chances against a kung-fu expert. How am I ever going to get myself out of this one?

I was deep in thought about the best way to fight off an attack from a Dragon Temple Guardian as I made my way Backstage.

"Hey, Donny, what do you know about Dragon Temple—"

"Mommy!" came a loud wail in Dragon. A flying object flew right into my face and sent me crashing to the floor. I landed on my butt with a painful thud and peeled Georgina off my face. Her wings tried to cling to me, and her claws grabbed at my

school shirt. *"Mommy! You back. You did leave me here all alone."*

"Yes, yes, I'm back," I said, gently prying her sharp claws from my shirt.

"Mommy, don't leave me again," Georgina wailed in my face. Golden snot streamed from her nose and golden tears gathered in her eyes like small pools of sunlight.

"Shhhh." I patted the little dragon on the head as she rested on my arm, perched there like a bird of prey.

Only Georgina isn't a bird of prey. She's a crying, whimpering dragon.

A blubbering dragon sobbing snot on my arm = 6 on the Feral Scale of Weirdness.

"She's been like this again all night," Donny said, looking tired. "She's been howling, crying. She won't sleep without you here."

"She misses her mommy," Red said with a roll of her eyes and a yawn. "Seriously, kid, as much as I don't want you snoring in the bed next to mine, I think you're going to have to move in if we ever want a good night's sleep again."

"I can't move in," I said simply.

"Well, then Georgina will have to go and live with you," Red replied.

"Negative." I shook my head. "No way is Mom letting me move into the zoo, and no way is she letting me keep a dragon as a pet. Even a housebroken one. I have another idea."

Donny looked at me skeptically. "And that is . . . ?"

There was a knock on the Backstage door.

"Ah, that will be my special delivery from China," Donny said brightly.

"Not another dragon egg, I hope," I muttered.

Donny swung open the door and found Mark standing on the doorstep. I'd almost forgotten that I'd asked him to meet me at the zoo before school—and to bring our secret weapon with him.

"Come in, Mark." I grinned. "I guess your special delivery is running late," I said to Donny. "What exactly are you expecting?"

"My new pet," Donny replied. "Don't worry," he added quickly, seeing the panic on my face. "It's not a dragon."

"Where do you want me to put the secret weapon?" Mark said, still standing on the doorstep.

Donny and Red gave me a puzzled look.

"Just bring it in here," I said.

The door opened wider and Mark struggled to drag a life-sized cardboard cutout of me into the room.

Red's mouth curled downward in disgust. "That is the most revolting thing I've ever—"

"Mommy!" Georgina wailed, flying off my arm

and right into the cutout. *"Two mommies?"* She looked confused.

"This mommy——" I pointed to myself *"——has to go to school today. So this mommy——"* I pointed to the life-sized cardboard version *"——is going to keep you company."*

"Mommy not leave me?" Georgina looked up at my cardboard face lovingly.

"This mommy's staying right here," I nodded.

"I'm used to seeing weird things," Donny smiled, "but a dragon thinking a cardboard cutout of a teenage boy is its mom is definitely a first."

"I printed it from my dad's computer and stuck it together using old cereal boxes," Mark said proudly.

"Anything that keeps Georgina quiet is fine by us," Donny said. "She's got a busy day ahead."

"Why?" I asked.

"We need to do a few tests on her," Donny replied.

Tests? On Georgina? I knew she wasn't really mine, but the thought of anything hurting her made my stomach tighten.

"Don't worry, the tests won't hurt," Donny reassured me. "But we do need to find out what kind of dragon she is."

"She's a Fire-Thrower," I said, confused.

"I'm not so sure," Donny replied. "But we'll know more after we've run the tests."

"Well, let me know if you discover something new!" I said. "That's if I survive the day of course. Did I forget to mention that I think someone is trying to kill me?"

Red pursed her painted black lips. "There's no need to be dramatic."

"I'm being followed by a Dragon Temple Guardian," I explained quickly.

Red sighed in frustration. "There's no such thing as the Dragon Temple!"

"Like there's no such thing as dragons,

yetis, werewolves, and wish frogs?" I said, annoyed.

Donny pulled a heavy-looking book from one of the shelves, blew the dust off it, and passed it to me. "Here—I forgot to tell you before that I have a book about the legend of the Dragon Temple. Half of it's written in Dragon so you'll be able to teach me a thing or two after you've read it. My Dragon is pretty basic."

I gave Georgina a goodbye pat on the head, thanked Donny for the book, and headed off to school with Mark.

"You really think that cardboard cutout will work until you get back?" Mark asked.

"Let's hope so. The last thing the zoo needs is a wailing dragon Backstage."

As soon as school was over I ran back home, finished off my homework, and then opened the book that Donny had given me. I read for hours and hours. The parts that were written in Dragon were easily the most interesting. I have loads to tell Donny when I next see him . . .

✱ The temple is over two thousand years old
✱ It's hidden away in the Chinese mountains and can only be accessed by flying dragons. (Maybe one day I could ride there on Georgina!)

* The temple is run by a man called Master Chow—a very wise old man
* The temple is guarded by kung-fu trained experts who call themselves the Dragon Temple Guardians
* Dragon Temple Guardians are some of the fiercest warriors known to man. They are trained from birth and can kill someone with just their little finger

I have as much power in my little finger as a sleeping sloth does on a sunny day.

There's no way I'd survive an attack from a Dragon Temple Guardian.

I'm dead meat for sure . . .

Thursday, March 5

Two mind-blowing things happened today:

1) The dragon test results are in—turns out
   Georgina isn't a Fire-Thrower after all!
2) Donny's new pet arrived from China

"Georgina is a very ancient and very rare subspecies
of dragon," Donny informed me, as I chomped
down my after-school cheese-and-pickle sandwich
in the Backstage offices. "She's what's known to us
cryptozoologists as a Golden Dreq."

"Bu dey're exint!" I spat sandwich out around
me as I spoke.

Georgina was fast asleep, nestled up again the Sammy Feral cardboard cutout. Weirdly, she seems to like the cardboard me more than the real me. Probably because the cardboard version doesn't tell her off for peeing indoors.

"Cryptozoology books might say that Golden Dreqs are extinct," Donny continued, "but they're wrong."

And then he told me exactly why Georgina was so amazing . . .

GOLDEN DREQ

* A subspecies of dragon only found in the remote highlands of China
* Thought to have died out years ago
* Can turn anything to gold with their fiery breath
* Their powers are only triggered once they hit puberty
* Georgina is most likely the last of her kind

Whoa! *What* now?

Georgina can turn things to gold?

No way!

"If Georgina *is* the last Golden Dreq dragon alive, then she's incredibly precious," Red pointed out.

"So whoever sent her to Feral Zoo," Donny added, "must want to keep her a secret and for us to keep her safe."

"And now the Dragon Temple Guardians want Georgina back," I said. "Maybe someone stole the egg from them and sent it to the zoo. Now they're following me around, waiting for the perfect moment to kill me so that they can steal the egg back!"

"If a Dragon Temple Guardian wanted you dead, then you'd be dead by now." Donny shrugged and scratched his head thoughtfully. "Did you have any luck with that book I lent you?"

"Yeah," I said. I quickly told him everything I'd read. "But if we really want to know more about the Dragon Temple Guardians, then we need to ask the pandas. And they've not exactly been that helpful till now . . ."

"Ah, well, we can use my new pet to tell if the pandas are lying or not," Donny said, giving me one of his rare smiles. He walked over to a tank in the corner of the room. The tank was covered with a black cloth, which Donny whipped away to reveal a large fish with long whiskers swimming about inside. The fish had beautiful scales which shimmered in the water like oil.

"That's your new pet?" I gasped. "What is it?"

"That," Donny said proudly, "is a truth trout—delivered last night straight from the Yangtze River in China. Truth trouts are amazing creatures," he continued, peering in at his new pet. "They can detect when people are telling lies—their scales turn red every time they hear a nontruth."

W.O.W!

I walked over to get a better look. "Say something untrue," Donny said.

"My name is Santa Claus," I said. I watched in amazement as the truth trout's oil-like scales began to glimmer in shades of blood red. "That is so cool," I whispered.

There was a sudden knock on the Backstage door. I spun around to see Max walking in.

Max is cool, and he knows just how weird

everything is Backstage, so we don't have to hide anything from him.

"Hey, guys." He waved at us. "Thought I'd stop by and see when I could get going on my new project."

Oh, rattlesnakes!

I'd totally and utterly forgotten that I promised Grace I'd help Max out.

"Studying Mongolian death worms again?" Donny asked him.

"Actually," Max said with a smile, bending down to the sleeping dragon curled up at the feet of my cardboard cutout, "I was hoping to study this little guy here."

"Sorry." Donny shook his head. "No can do. Georgina isn't available for observation at the moment. But you're welcome to study any of my other pets if you like. In fact I have a new addition to my collection . . ." Donny looked over at the truth trout proudly.

Never mind the truth trout—there was a species of animal in Feral Zoo that was way more weird . . .

"Why don't you study the pandas, Max?" I said loudly.

"Great idea, Sammy," Donny agreed.

"Um . . ." Max looked confused. "I know pandas are rare, but I was hoping to get a scoop on something REALLY rare, if you get my drift."

"Trust me, Max," I said. "Pandas are as weird as a wonky winkle clam. I bet there's loads of stuff we don't know about them."

"What makes you think that pandas are weird?" Max said, looking unconvinced.

"I can speak their language," I told him.

This got Max's attention.

"And the pandas are always going on about how 'special' they are. You can be the one to find out exactly what that means . . ."

Max's face lit up.

The more I think about it, the more I wonder what the pandas mean by "special."

Can they breathe underwater? Can they fly? Can they fight off kids who can kill you with their little finger? Because right now, that would be *really* useful.

Friday, March 6

Mission for today = catch the boy who's out to kill me!

I don't care if he's a Dragon Temple Guardian.

I don't care if he's super-strong and super-fast and could kill me with his little finger.

And I don't care how good he might be at hiding. Today is the day I am going to expose him!

I am PSYCHED UP and ready to go.

Sammy Feral vs. Dragon Temple Guardian!

If I die, then I'll die fighting!

Will report back later . . .

LATER

I spent my whole journey to school keeping an eye out for dragon-boy. Every time I walked past a tree, I expected him to leap karate-chopping out of it, and with every step I took, I expected him to jump out in front of me—ready to land a fatal blow. But there was no sign. I looked for him at school, but no luck there either.

After school I looked around every corner with a mirror, studied every stranger I saw, in case the boy was in disguise, and even went the long way home to try to trick him. But there was no sign of him anywhere.

I was psyched up and ready to face him, but he was nowhere to be seen.

Disappointed, I let myself into the house and headed straight up to my bedroom. I was too annoyed to even fix myself an after-school snack—and I'm always hungry after school!

As I got to the top of the stairs I heard a funny noise coming from behind my bedroom door. Someone was in my room.

"Natty, if that's you looking for my secret cookie stash again, I'm going to . . ." I pushed the door open and froze in horror.

Natty wasn't standing in my bedroom.

It was the boy.

The Dragon Temple Guardian.

And he was holding my diary.

I froze, and suddenly all the fight I had in me vanished and all I could think was that I didn't want to die.

He looked about my age. He was my height with short black hair and wore a black-belted kung-fu outfit. And he might as well have had the words DON'T MESS WITH ME tattooed across his forehead.

This is it, I thought. He's come here to kill me . . .

"You're a Dragon Temple Guardian," I whispered.

The boy didn't say anything. He just narrowed his eyes at me.

"Why are you following me?" I asked, taking a step toward him, trying to be brave. "Do you want to kill me?"

He held up my diary and waved it, giving me the tiniest of smiles.

Then, in a blink of an eye, the boy darted toward my open bedroom window and leaped through it.

I stood there, stunned by what I'd just seen.

He hadn't tried to kill me. He'd broken into my house and stolen my diary!

This was WAR!

I ran to the window and looked out. I scanned the garden and the world beyond, but there was no sign of the boy. He'd literally vanished into thin air.

Dragon Temple Guardian = 1, Sammy Feral = 0.

My plan to catch the spying Dragon Temple Guardian had been as successful as a naked mole rat running for beauty queen.

But no one follows me and gets away with it.

No one breaks into my house and gets away with it.

And no one—NO ONE—steals my diary and smirks at me as they take off with it!

I'm writing this on a scrap of paper torn out of my school English workbook. I'll stick it into my diary as soon as I get it back. And I WILL get it back! I am going to find this dragon-boy, and I am going to discover what he wants once and for all!

Saturday, March 7

"So you're saying the boy just broke into your house, crept into your room, and stole your diary. Then he leaped out of your bedroom window and vanished?"

"That's right," I said to Donny.

Donny, Red, the wish frog, and I were standing in the Backstage yard watching Grace trying to train Georgina to fly in low circles.

"I still think you should tell Mom and Dad about this," Grace said over her shoulder, putting out a gloved hand for Georgina to perch on. "They should know how easy the house is to break into."

"No way." I shook my head. "They cannot know about any of this. And it's not easy to break into— that guy's a ninja!"

"Well, at least we know one thing for sure," Red said. "You're not going crazy. You really were being followed."

The wish frog leaped from Red's shoulder onto mine. "Is there anything in your diary, Sammy, that we wouldn't want the world to know about?"

Hmmm, let me think . . . My family are ex-werewolves, I can talk to animals that supposedly don't exist, I once helped rescue a yeti chief and destroy the Hell Hound . . .

"Let's just say that whoever reads that diary will have a LOT of dirt on all of us," I said, shaking my head.

"Well, it's gone, and there's nothing we can do about it," Donny said with a sigh. "Besides, we have bigger things to worry about at the moment."

"Like the fact that Georgina is growing bigger by the day and it's going to be hard to keep her a secret for much longer," Grace said.

"And we still don't know why she's been sent to the zoo," I pointed out.

"And the fact that Friday the 13th is less than a week away," Red added.

Er, Friday the 13th? What did that have to do with anything?

"Friday the 13th is a very powerful day for weird animals," Donny explained, reading my puzzled expression. "Once the sun begins to set on that date, their powers are heightened. They can become aggressive and territorial."

Brilliant. That's just what we need right now. NOT.

"I suggest we reinforce the zoo," Red said. "We'll need to put your family in a cage and put the wish frog, the phoenix, and Georgina under extra-special protection."

Before I could say anything my phone buzzed in my pocket.

It was Max. "Hey, Sammy," he said. "That boy you told me to look out for in the zoo—the one in the kung-fu outfit—he's here. By the panda enclosure."

I snapped my phone shut. "Gotta go," I said. This battle was between me and the dragon-boy—if I could keep the others safe then I would. However, there was one person I needed to help me . . . "Red, I need you."

Red rolled her eyes and crossed her arms, giving me one of her famous death stares.

"Please—it's important," I added.

"Fine," she huffed.

Red and I left Backstage and headed into the main zoo, toward the panda enclosure. "The Dragon Temple Guardian is here in the zoo," I told her as we hurried along. "We need to try to trick him Backstage and into one of the cages."

Red grabbed me and swung me around to

face her. "You should have warned everyone! He's dangerous!"

"I can handle this!" I wriggled out of her gasp. "But I need you to help me."

Red grimaced for a moment before nodding reluctantly.

As we turned the corner to the panda enclosure I saw him standing there, peering through the glass at them. The corner of my diary was poking out of his back pocket.

"Red," I whispered, "I need you to float my diary out of his pocket and dangle it in front of his face . . ."

Red gave me a mischievous grin. "I know exactly where you're going with this," she winked.

Without moving a muscle, Red levitated my diary out of the boy's back pocket using only the power of her mind. She dangled it in front of his face and he looked at it in horror. As he moved his hands to try to snatch the diary back, Red quickly whipped it away and floated it through the air in front of him.

The boy began to chase the diary through the zoo, like a fish following bait.

Using Red's amazing ability, we made the boy follow the flying diary away from the panda enclosure, past the lion den and the polar bears, through the monkey enclosure, and toward the Backstage gates.

Red unlocked the gates with her mind and floated the diary through them. The boy ran after it desperately.

Red and I ran in after him, locking the gates behind us.

The boy didn't have time to see the others standing in the yard before Red floated the diary into one of the old werewolf cages. Just as the boy's gaze fell on Georgina, who was perched on Grace's arm, he ran into the werewolf cage and the door slammed shut behind him.

"Haha!" I punched the air with joy.

Red high-fived me before floating the diary between the cage bars and into my hands.

I grabbed it and held it close to my chest.

Man, it was good to have it back again.

And it was even better to see the mysterious boy locked up in a werewolf enclosure!

He grabbed the cage bars between his hands

and narrowed his eyes in anger. "Sammy Feral," he growled at me.

"Who are you, and why have you been following me?" I demanded, taking a step toward him.

He smirked at me. "Your diary makes for excellent bedtime reading. Who would have thought that the wish frog was still alive and living at Feral Zoo!"

"You wrote about me in your diary?" the wish frog said angrily.

"That diary is private property!" I shouted at the boy. "You had no right—"

"Relax." He raised a hand. "Your secrets are safe with me. I came here to give you the diary back."

"Why did you take it in the first place?" Donny asked.

"I needed to know if I could trust you," the boy replied. "You are, after all, looking after the last ever Golden Dreq dragon."

"Was it you who sent Georgina to Feral Zoo?" Red asked. "Or have you come here to kill us all?"

The boy shook his head. "The master of the

Dragon Temple, Master Chow, sent the egg here. The Dragon Temple was no longer safe."

"So you really are a Dragon Temple Guardian," I whispered, amazed.

The boy nodded. "My name is Bruce. It is my destiny—as it is the destiny of all Dragon Temple Guardians—to protect and preserve the dying race of dragons. Master Chow sent me here to make sure that Georgina is in the safest place she can be. She needs to be with people we can trust."

"So you're not here to kill me?"

Bruce shook his head. "The very opposite—I need your help."

Phew!

"Who are we protecting Georgina from?" I asked, taking another step toward Bruce.

"A terrible, terrible evil," he whispered, gripping the cage bars even more tightly. "The Dragon Temple is nearly as old as mankind. As long as man has known about dragons, those of us at the temple have sworn to give our lives to protect them. And never in our thousands of years of history have we seen an evil like the one who wishes to enslave Georgina."

I looked over at Georgina, my heart thumping loudly in my chest.

Someone wants to enslave her?

Thank goodness she couldn't understand English. There was no way I wanted her to hear a word that Bruce was saying.

"Sammy Feral," Bruce said in a low voice, "you and your friends must be ready to battle and lay down your lives so that Georgina can survive. You must be ready to face the terrible Mysterious Mistress X."

Whoa, rewind!

Why does everything always have to be about fighting to the death?

"The Mysterious Mistress X?" I repeated. "What kind of name is that?"

"She is a wicked, wicked woman," Bruce said gravely. "So selfish and cruel. She cares only for herself and for material wealth. That evil woman will only be happy when she owns every last scrap of gold in the world. It is because of her that the Golden Dreq dragons have all but died out. It is her fault alone that Georgina is the last of her kind."

The others came closer to the cage so we could listen to the story that Bruce needed to tell us.

"Mysterious Mistress X spent years tracking down every Golden Dreq dragon in the world," Bruce continued. "Soon she had enslaved hundreds of them. She chained them up in a cold, damp basement and made them breathe onto piles of trash to turn it into gold. While the dragons went hungry she sat on golden chairs at golden tables and ate from pure gold plates. She wore golden-thread clothes and slept in a golden bed while the poor dragons were forced to sleep on the hard ground. Eventually the dragons died, one by one, but there was one brave dragon who survived Mysterious Mistress X's cruelty.

"That dragon was so brave, so strong in spirit, that no matter how cruel and wicked Mysterious Mistress X was, she survived. That one dragon, after years of mistreatment, managed to escape her prison and fly on crooked wings all the way back to China. She flew to the Dragon Temple and there we were able to nurse her back to health. After years of cruel captivity she never regained her full strength, but she did fall in love with another dragon at the temple. The last thing she did before she died was lay an egg."

"Georgina," I said quietly. The dragon that had escaped Mysterious Mistress X was Georgina's mother.

Bruce nodded his head. "Georgina is only a half-breed Golden Dreq, but her powers will come to her someday. And when they do, Mysterious Mistress X will surely come after her."

"No way," I growled. "We will protect Georgina with our lives. There's no way Mysterious Mistress X will ever take her and treat her as badly as she treated those other dragons."

"I'm glad I can trust you." Bruce nodded happily.

"Oh, you can trust us," Donny reassured him.

"We're the best people in the world to protect Georgina," Red agreed.

"We won't let any harm come to her," the wish frog added.

"And if Mysterious Mistress X should ever come looking for Georgina," I said, "then we'll be ready."

Sunday, March 8

We eventually let Bruce out of the werewolf cage yesterday. But not before we made him tell us the whole story again—only this time we had the truth trout listen to him.

Bruce is definitely telling the truth.

Mysterious Mistress X is real, and so is the Dragon Temple.

And Georgina is in terrible danger.

"What kind of a name is Mysterious Mistress X anyway?" I said as we all gathered in the Backstage offices this morning.

Donny had called an emergency meeting and EVERYONE was there (well, apart from Mom and Dad). Me, Donny, Red, Mark, the wish frog, Natty, Grace, and Max, all crammed into the Backstage offices. Georgina slept curled up at the feet of my cardboard cutout, and the rest of us squeezed in between the tanks housing Donny's weird pets.

Donny quickly recapped everything that had happened yesterday.

"So where's Bruce now?" Mark asked.

"Now he knows he can trust us, he's gone back to China to report to Master Chow," I told him.

"I still don't understand why Feral Zoo is safer for Georgina than this Dragon Temple," Max said.

"The Dragon Temple is the first place Mysterious Mistress X will look," Donny explained. "Here at Feral Zoo we have a better chance of keeping her safe."

"But if Mistress X does find her way to Feral Zoo," Grace said, "how will we keep Georgina safe? I've trained her to fly in low circles and pee outside, but I can't train her to disguise herself as something other than a dragon."

"Maybe we could cover her with feathers and disguise her as some kind of bird of prey?" Mark suggested.

"A bird of prey that breathes fire?" Red said skeptically.

"There's no hiding the fact that Georgina is a dragon." Donny scratched his head. "But if Mysterious Mistress X does discover Georgina's living at the zoo, we need to convince her that she's not a Golden Dreq dragon, and that she has no use for her. But how do we do that?"

"We could paint her?" Natty suggested.

Grace shook her head. "I'm not sure that's—"

"A great idea!" Donny, Red, and I said at once.

"If Georgina is any other color than gold, then we might have a chance of convincing whoever finds her that she isn't a Golden Dreq. Her powers haven't been activated yet, so there's no other way to know what kind of dragon she is without doing further tests," Donny added. "Okay, guys, this is what we'll do . . ."

Everyone listened carefully as Donny dished out jobs:

* Natty, Grace, and Mark—spray-paint Georgina another color
* Sammy—do some research into Mysterious Mistress X
* Max—continue to study the pandas in case they can help us
* Donny, Red, and the wish frog—prepare the zoo for Friday the 13th

I've spent most of the day reading Donny's library of cryptozoology books while the others are busy with their own jobs. But it's difficult trying to research someone whose real name you don't even know. I mean, what does the "X" in Mysterious Mistress X even stand for? X-treme, X-aggerated, X-asperating, X-ceptionally cruel?

The Internet came up with a big fat nothing, and after nearly a full day of reading Donny's books I still have no new info!

"Mommy," came a small voice from the Backstage office doorway.

I looked up from *Dragons and Their Foes* to see a bright red dragon looking back at me.

I smiled. *"Georgina, you have a new coat."*

Wow, they'd done a very good job of painting her.

Georgina waddled over to me and snuggled into my lap. She fell asleep, and her little scaly face looked so peaceful—how could anyone want to harm her?

Whoever this Mysterious Mistress X really is, she'll have to fight me to the death before she lays a finger on Georgina!

Monday, March 9
4 days until Friday the 13th

I went to the zoo right after school today. Donny and Red have spent the whole day reinforcing all the cages Backstage in preparation for Friday the 13th.

FRIDAY THE 13TH

* Considered to be an unlucky day
* Fear of Friday the 13th is called friggatriskaidekaphobia. (Try to say that quickly!)
* The power of weird animals grows stronger after the sun sets on Friday the 13th
* This coming Friday the 13th is also a full moon . . . Yikes!

"Has anyone ever told you you're friggatriskaidekaphobic?" I asked Donny as we both watched Red reinforce the gut worm's cage with a stick of metal and a soldering iron. She wasn't holding either object of course—she was controlling them with her mind.

"Where did you learn that word?" Donny asked me.

"From reading one of your books."

"You're meant to be researching Mysterious Mistress X," he said. "Not Friday the 13th."

"Mysterious Mistress X is so mysterious there's basically nothing written on her anywhere. I don't have anything new to report. And I can't help but think you're being a bit paranoid about this whole Friday the 13th thing. I mean, it's just superstition, right?"

"Wrong," Red answered, dropping the metal bar to the ground with a clang. "Friday the 13th is as weird as it gets—you'll see for yourself soon enough."

"I spoke to your dad today," Donny told me. "He's considering shutting the zoo for the weekend because of it."

"You can't make him do that!" I said. "We've got loads of visitors at the moment—way more than normal because they're coming to see the pandas. Think of all the people who'll be disappointed if the zoo is shut for the weekend."

"And think of all the people whose lives will be in danger if we can't manage to control all the weird creatures we have living here this Friday."

Fair point.

"Look, Sammy—" Donny turned to me, "— you worry about Mysterious Mistress X, and let us worry about Friday the 13th, okay?"

What choice do I have?

I left the zoo in a sulk and spent the rest of the evening shut up in my room eating toast and feeling sorry for myself.

Why do I always get the dumb, dead-end jobs? Why do I have to research someone as mysterious as the Bermuda Triangle? Can't I spray-paint dragons and research pandas instead?

Life is SO unfair sometimes!

Wednesday, March 11
2 days until Friday the 13th

The zoo has been mega-busy all week—lots of people are coming here to see Cheng and Su. And in between sweeping out their enclosure and making sure they've got enough fresh bamboo to eat, I've been trying to pick their panda brains . . .

It feels as if it might be easier to fly on the wings of a cranky crow than it is to get information out of a panda. But I do believe they know a lot more than they let on. They knew about dragons and about Dragon Temple Guardians, and I'd bet my crocodile-tooth collection that they know a thing or two about Mysterious Mistress X!

And just to make sure they told me nothing but the truth, Donny let me take the truth trout with me when I paid them a visit.

"We don't eat fish, freckles," Cheng huffed at me when I came into their enclosure with the truth trout in a portable tank.

"This isn't here for you to eat," I told them. *"It's here to make sure you're telling me the truth when I ask you a few questions."*

"Questions about what?" Su raised his fuzzy eyebrows. *"About what makes us so special? Isn't that what your friend Max is trying to work out too?"*

"I want to know everything you can tell me about Mysterious Mistress X."

I sat with the truth trout on my lap, watching as it turned various shades of angry red as the pandas began to talk.

"She once performed in the Russian ballet," Cheng said. *"And she loves kittens."*

"You're lying to me." I pointed at the truth trout. *"Truth only, or you'll be on the first plane back to China . . ."*

So the pandas talked some more, and this time the truth trout flashed brilliant shades of blue as they told me the truth about Mysterious Mistress X.

Check out these interesting facts about her . . .

MYSTERIOUS MISTRESS X

* **Lives:** In a castle made of gold in Russia
* **Looks like:** A mega-rich queen draped in golden fur and dripping in gold jewelry
* **Army:** She uses her gold to employ a ruthless army to do her dirty work
* **Obsession:** Gold, dragons, money, more gold

"*Just one more thing,*" I said, as I turned to go. "*Is it true that weird animals become weirder on Friday the 13th?*"

I held the truth trout in front of me and waited for their reply.

"*As weird as a wildebeest on a waterslide, freckles,*" Cheng replied.

I knew he was telling the truth when the truth trout flashed a bright blue.

Great, only two more days before the Feral Scale of Weirdness skyrockets once again . . .

Thursday, March 12
1 day until Friday the 13th

Not only is there only one more day before Friday the 13th, but the full moon started today.

Being ex-werewolves, my family gets SUPER-stressed around the full moon. Excessive ear hair, bad tempers, and a freakishly good sense of smell are the regular symptoms they suffer from. But there's no denying it . . . this month they seem a lot worse.

* I caught Dad on all fours in the wolf enclosure after school today, drinking out of their water tank

* I found Grace and Natty shaving each other's back hair in the bathroom this evening (and it was WAY longer than normal). GROSS!

* Mom came back from the butcher's with nothing but pig feet and lamb eyes for dinner—she totally forgot to bring me any normal food

* Caliban's been howling at the moon ALL NIGHT LONG!

And it's not just my ex-werewolf family that is acting extra-weird. Tomorrow being Friday the 13th is affecting every weird creature in the zoo.

✱ Georgina has been breathing a lot more fire than usual. Donny has taken to following her around with a fire extinguisher

✱ The pandas are being EVEN GRUMPIER than normal, and they've started sneezing a lot. (Or maybe they're just getting a cold—who knows?)

* The phoenix has burst into flames twice in
  two days

* The wish frog is refusing to come out of
  his tank because hc's so frightened he'll
  accidentally grant someone a wish

"Donny's right," I heard Dad say to Mom quietly this
evening. "We need to close the zoo this weekend.
It's too dangerous to allow members of the public
anywhere near us at the moment."

"I agree," Mom said.

"We'll tell the children that we're spending

the weekend at the zoo. We'll have to sleep in the werewolf cages, and let's just hope Sammy, Donny, and Red can keep everything else under control."

So it's up to me, Donny, and Red to make sure the weird animals at the zoo—including my family— don't escape and create havoc this weekend. PLUS we need to worry about Mysterious Mistress X— she could come to the zoo at any time and try to take Georgina from us. At least I could recognize her now the pandas have given me a description of her. If any spoiled-looking Russian queens come within a mile of me, then they'll be sorry.

Tomorrow is going to be one big wacko party . . . bring it on!

Friday the 13th

While Donny and Red spent the day getting the last few things sorted out Backstage in preparation for sundown, I headed to the main zoo right after school to help out with the Friday the 13th–themed activities.

Dad compromised and decided to keep the zoo open during the day but closed it early, giving people time to get as far away as possible before the sun set.

Mark and I swung by the zoo café to pick up snacks before checking out some of the cool Friday the 13th activities.

* Max gave a talk on vampire bats. (Did you know that they shave the hair off their victims with their razor-sharp teeth before they bite and drain their blood?!)
* Grace did a "Deadly Animals Tour" of the zoo
* Mom had arranged for a photographer to come in and take pictures of people with Betty the boa constrictor
* Dad, with Caliban at his heels, welcomed a journalist from the local newspaper into the Rare Animal Breeding Center and gave him a guided tour

"It's such a shame you're closing the zoo early today, Mr. Feral," said the journalist as Dad showed him out.

"I'm afraid we have some essential zoo maintenance to see to this weekend," Dad replied politely. "We can't keep winning 'Zoo of the Year' without it!" He chuckled nervously.

As the last of the visitors left the zoo, and the big metal gates locked behind them, everyone breathed a heavy sigh of relief.

"I thought some of them would never leave," Grace complained.

"We don't have much time before the sun sets," Mom said. "I think we'll need to eat dinner in our cages."

So my family and Caliban and Max (who's also an ex-werewolf) all headed Backstage and let me lock them in the newly reinforced cages. I pushed their dinners of raw steak and french fries through the bars as the last of the evening's sun slipped below the horizon.

"It's showtime, kid," Red whispered in my ear. "You ready?"

I gave her a winning smile. "I was born ready."

I wasn't sure what to expect as the sky grew darker and the air grew colder.

Then I heard a deep growling noise coming from the werewolf cages . . . It was Dad.

He curled his lip and snarled at me as his back began to hunch, and dark, thick hair sprouted all over his body. I watched in horror as he sank to all fours, his clothes were shredded, and a tail grew out of the base of his spine.

Mom was next to transform. She howled at the moon as soon as she was in wolf form. Grace, Max, Natty, and Caliban quickly followed, and soon six deadly werewolves were trapped behind the cage bars instead of my family.

I hadn't seen them in full werewolf form since they had been cured of the were-virus.

"It's only because it's Friday the 13th, Sammy," Red said gently, as if reading my mind.

I walked away before my were-family had a chance to tell me how good I'd taste in a burger bun. "Let's go inside," I shouted over my shoulder at Red. "No way do I want to stick around and watch this freak show out here!"

Did I think the scene in the Backstage offices wouldn't be a freak show?

Has someone pulled out my brains through my nose and replaced them with stewed spaghetti?

The scene Backstage had sent the Feral Scale of Weirdness into orbit!

The phoenix was bursting into flames and then hatching from an egg over and over again, each cycle taking no longer than a few minutes.

The gut worm was thrashing around violently inside his cage, trying to burst out and attack us with all three heads.

Donny stood next to the fire-breathing turtle's tank with a fire extinguisher, blasting the animal with slippery foam every few seconds as it tried to incinerate everything around it.

In the corner of the room a small box jumped up and down like some kind of jumping bean. "What's going on there?" I asked, pointing at the box.

"The wish frog insisted on locking himself away so he wouldn't be tempted to grant any wishes," Donny said, spraying the fire-breathing turtle with wet foam once again.

"We've moved the pandas into the room next door. We're still not sure what their power is, but we thought it best to keep an eye on them."

"Good idea."

But worse than the sight of the violently thrashing gut worm, the rainbow of colors of the truth trout and the constant rebirth of the phoenix was the noise they were all making.

I could hear every one of them shouting and screaming at the top of their lungs. The words blurred together into one freakish symphony of sound. It was almost too much to bear.

I clamped my hands over my ears and shut my eyes for a moment. What could I do? Go outside and be confronted by my were-family? Or stay inside and let myself be deafened by this racket?

"Sammy, Sammy!" I felt someone tugging on my arm. I peeped one eye open to see Red staring at me in horror.

"What?" I shouted back.

"Where's Georgina?"

Good point!

I looked around wildly—Georgina was nowhere to be seen.

"Quick, let's check next door!"

Red and I ran into the next room and nearly collapsed in shock at what we saw.

Everything had been turned to gold. The furniture, the books, the walls, the camp beds that Donny and Red slept on. The pandas were nowhere to be seen. And in the middle of the room, burping up fire and turning the floor around her into solid gleaming gold, was Georgina.

"Sorry, Mommy. Fire bad, but me can't help it."

"My computer!" Red screamed, picking up her now useless gold laptop. "Georgina's destroyed everything!"

"Destroyed is not the word I would choose," said a voice with a strong Russian accent from the corner of the room.

My blood froze in my veins.

"How could turning something to gold ever be destruction?" came the voice again. It was as gravelly as a grave. A figure stepped out of the shadows: a thin woman in a sharp golden suit. She was wearing gold-rimmed sunglasses and a golden fox fur wrapped around her neck (YUCK!). Her golden hair was tied tightly behind her head and she wore an expression of pure triumph. I watched in horror as she bent down and scooped Georgina up into her arms.

"Mysterious Mistress X!" I gasped. "How did you find us?"

"You typed my name into Google," she smirked. "I like to keep an eye on people who want to know about me, so I decided to come here and check you out. All I had to do was locate your computer and track you down. I'm so glad that I did—I've been searching for this dragon ever since I heard its useless mother had laid an egg. I've spent weeks trying to find it. I searched the Dragon Temple, and when it wasn't there I knew it had been sent away somewhere it would be kept hidden from me. I've tortured every dragon breeder, every cryptozoologist, and every zookeeper I could find to try to squeeze information out of them. But in the end it was you, Sammy Feral, who led me straight here . . ."

Uh-oh . . .

"Donny!" Red shouted. "Come quick!"

"At first I thought you had a Coral-breed

dragon living at your zoo," Mysterious Mistress X continued, looking down at Georgina greedily and licking her lips. "With her pretty red scales and her red claws. But something wasn't quite right. I thought tonight would be my chance. Friday the 13th—if the dragon was a Golden Dreq, then its powers would be revealed at sunset."

"YOU!" shouted Donny as he entered the room. The fire extinguisher was still in his hands. "How did you find us?"

Mysterious Mistress X was distracted, looking at Donny. I lunged forward and snatched Georgina out of her grasp.

Suddenly smoke billowed into the room and there was the sound of roaring flames.

"The fire-breathing turtle!" I screamed. "It's setting the place alight!"

Donny ran from the room with the fire extinguisher in his hands as Mysterious

190

Mistress X launched herself at me and made a grab for Georgina. Red picked up the golden laptop with her mind and hurled it through the air toward the evil woman's head. It hit her square on with a loud *thunk* and she staggered backward.

There was another loud whoosh of flames.

I ran from the room, Georgina safely in my arms.

The room next door was being eaten up by fire. The cages had been destroyed and Donny's pets were flapping and writhing free.

It was pandemonium!

As Donny and Red struggled to contain the chaos, Mysterious Mistress X stumbled into the room.

She was holding something in her hands. For a moment I couldn't see what it was, and then I suddenly understood.

It was a gun.

I'd never seen a gun in real life before—only on TV and in films. This gun was golden and it made a clicking noise as she pulled back the safety catch.

"Give me the dragon, Sammy, or I'll shoot you dead."

This was it. I'd promised Bruce that I'd fight to the death for Georgina. And it looked as if I was about to follow through on that promise.

I'd got myself out of a lot of sticky situations before—but dodging a bullet wasn't one of them.

My hands tightened around Georgina and I prepared to take the blast of the gun, when from the corner of my eye I saw a three-headed snake writhe toward Mysterious Mistress X.

"Attack her!" I shouted at the gut worm, and it licked its lips at the sight of the woman who was about to kill me. *"Attack!"*

Without a moment's pause the gut worm launched itself at the evil villain. Its jaws sank into her arm. She dropped the golden gun and screamed a blood-curdling scream as she tried to fight the creature off.

In the haze of smoke and ash that billowed through the air I watched as she fought the three-headed beast with everything she had. Suddenly the gut worm was on the ground and Mysterious Mistress X had gone.

She'd escaped.

"Red, take Georgina!" I passed the little dragon to her and sprinted out the door.

I followed the trail of blood on the ground.

In the darkness I could see the figure of a woman limping toward the Backstage gates, running for her life.

"Don't come back!" I warned her. "You're lucky to be leaving here alive—next time you won't be so fortunate!"

"Next time you won't see me hesitate to shoot!" she shouted back. "I know where you are, Sammy, and I know that the Golden Dreq dragon is here too. I'll be back—I can promise you that."

The sounds of my werewolf family howling

and Donny trying to contain the blaze filled the air as Mysterious Mistress X slipped away into the darkness.

Saturday, March 14

Dear Sammy Feral,
There are no bars strong enough.
No fires hot enough. No gut worms
crazed enough. There is nothing that
will keep me away from Feral Zoo
and away from the Dreq.
     Next time I come, I will not hesitate
to kill you if you get in my way.

Mysterious Mistress X

I hung my head in my hands and for the hundredth time I reread the letter that had appeared at the zoo this morning.

Thank heavens Dad decided to close the zoo today. We need everyone Backstage, cleaning up the carnage left by Friday the 13th.

Every animal cage, tank, and enclosure was destroyed and has to be remade from scratch. Georgina's red-paint disguise had washed off in the chaos of trying to put out the fires last night—and there's no point in repainting her now that Mysterious Mistress X knows she's here.

Dad and Max went to the hardware store early this morning and stocked up on wood, nails, metal bars, and anything else that could be used to rehouse the weird animals.

The rest of us spent the morning trying to recapture everything that had escaped.

Thankfully nothing had left the zoo. We found the phoenix asleep by the vulture aviary, the gut worm curled up in a python tank, and the fire-breathing turtle had managed to sneak into the Komodo dragon enclosure and spend the night there.

Weirdly, as soon as the sun came up we found the pandas sitting in the charred Backstage office—where they'd last been seen last night.

"We've been here the whole time," Cheng said when I asked her. And I knew that she was telling the truth as the truth trout was listening in. *"You just couldn't see us."*

Suddenly, the penny dropped. *"That's what makes pandas so special, isn't it?"* I said, excitement rising inside me. *"You can become invisible!"*

"Like we said before," Cheng said with a smile, *"you've spent all this time asking about dragons and not once asked about us pandas . . ."*

"How?" I asked. *"How come I can see you now and I couldn't last night?"*

"Beats me." Cheng shrugged. I quickly looked over at the truth trout, who was still glistening blue. Cheng was telling the truth—she really had no idea how pandas turned invisible.

Well, I was going to find out!

Later, as we scrubbed the ash off Donny's bookshelves, I told Max all about pandas turning invisible. The fire had destroyed a lot of books, the curtains, and most of the furniture Backstage, but thankfully the building itself was still standing.

"It's an interesting theory, Sammy," Max agreed. "I'll look into it."

"Not a theory," I told him. "They really can turn invisible. If you can work out how, then you'll be doing something no one's ever done before!"

Max grinned from ear to ear. "Cool!"

Thankfully my family was back to normal this morning. I say "normal"; they still have some lingering werewolf symptoms—Mom was able to find the phoenix in the vulture aviary just by sniffing him out—but the main thing is, they're human again.

Today was more tiring than swimming through sea sludge. When I wasn't trying to sort out the mess Backstage I was worrying about how we were going to keep Georgina safe now that Mysterious Mistress X has found her secret hiding place.

"I don't know, Sammy," Donny said, looking worried. "Let's talk about it tomorrow, once we've all had some time to think."

"She looked pretty injured," Red added. "The gut worm bit her quite badly. I don't think she'll be back for Georgina until she's healed."

"I just don't know how Georgina can ever be safe at the zoo now," I said.

"Maybe she can't," Donny said quietly. "But one

thing's for sure, now that her powers have been activated, we have to work harder than ever to protect her." Donny exchanged a knowing look with Red.

I know that look. I've seen it before. It's a look that says they know something that I don't. They're plotting something and they haven't let me in on the secret.

No way.

Georgina thinks I'm her mother. She's my responsibility.

I'll do anything to keep her safe—even die for her if I have to.

If they have a plan, then I'm going to be a part of it, no matter what.

Sunday, March 15

I hardly slept last night. After a showdown with Mom where I had no choice but to tell her all about Georgina, she finally let me bring the tiny dragon back home.

"At least here you'll be safe," I told Georgina. *"That horrible woman thinks you're at the zoo, not in my bedroom. But you HAVE to behave while you're here."*

"No fire or pee-pee in house," Georgina said proudly.

"That's right." I patted her head. *"Good dragon."*

I spent the whole night watching Georgina

sleep and trying to think of ways to keep her safe. She's such a cute, innocent little thing. She doesn't deserve to be captured and enslaved by some wicked gold-obsessed she-devil. I may not really be Georgina's mother, but I would do anything to keep her safe.

Georgina and I traveled to the zoo early this morning while it was still dark outside.

I found Donny and Red in the charred Backstage offices. They were both packing bags.

"You're leaving?" I said in shock. "You can't. We need you here to help keep Georgina safe."

"So long as Georgina is here, she won't be safe," Donny said, zipping up his suitcase.

"We're leaving and we're taking her with us," Red said.

Oh no, you're not!

"Well, then I'm coming with you!" I shouted, clenching my fists.

"Sammy, your family needs you here," Donny said gently. "And I can't take all my pets with me—I need someone here to look after them."

"Mark can do it," I said quickly. "He's actually really good with them. And my family will understand that I had to go away to keep Georgina safe. They won't miss me, and I'll be back soon . . ."

"That's the thing, Sammy," Red said. "We might never be able to come back."

"So long as we're here—so long as Georgina's here—then the zoo and everyone in it is in danger," Donny said. "It's not fair to the animals or your family or the other people who work here. Not to mention the visitors! It's safer for everyone this way."

"Don't worry," Red said, lifting Georgina out of my arms and stroking her head. "We'll take good care of her."

I was silent for a moment.

For a split second I thought about what life at the zoo would be like without Donny and Red. No more cryptozoology lessons, no more weird pets being brought home. No more crazy killers or animal-obsessed lunatics to have to do battle with. Life might even be . . . peaceful.

But a peaceful life = not for me!

Not if peaceful means someone else is doing all the hard work and protecting animals from crazy people like Mysterious Mistress X. I can't ignore the fact that people like her exist. I can't turn my back on the fight for crypto-justice and pretend that evil doesn't exist.

Evil does exist—and it's my job to fight it.

"We're in this together," I said slowly, taking a deep breath and meaning every word I said, "and I'll do anything to keep Georgina and animals like her safe. Even if that means leaving the zoo and my family and everything I love."

Donny nodded his head. "Okay. Pack light—once we're on the run then we'll need to keep running until we find a way to defeat Mysterious Mistress X. Say your goodbyes, Sammy. We leave tonight."

How do you say goodbye to your family knowing that you may never see them again?

I just couldn't bring myself to do it.

Instead I spent the day hanging out at the zoo, pretending everything was normal. If today was the last time I ever saw my family, then I wanted happy memories to hold on to.

* I helped Mom groom the llamas and helped Natty feed the penguins
* I helped translate the pandas for Max and Grace as Max continued his

project and tried to work out how
they had become invisible on Friday
the 13th

✱ I took Caliban for an extra-long walk and
ate lunch with Dad in the zoo café.

✱ I hung out with Mark in the reptile
house and spent time with my pet
python Beelzebub

✱ I enjoyed my family dinner this
evening, knowing it could be my
last. And as everyone started to brush
their teeth for bed, I even told my mom I
loved her

She smiled at me. "Are you okay, Sammy?"

I shook my head. "I'm just glad I have the best
family in the world."

After everyone had gone to bed, I hurriedly
packed a bag and wrote my family a note, which I
left on my pillow.

Dear Mom, Dad, Grace, Natty, and Caliban,

I mean it when I say you're the best family anyone could ever ask for. I'm sorry I don't tell you often enough.

I'm going away—it's for your own good. So long as I'm at the zoo with Georgina, then none of you are safe.

I hope you understand.

One day, if it's safe for me to come back, then I will. I promise.

Please don't forget me. I will never forget about you.

Sammy

P.S. Please can you ask Mark to look after Donny's pets?

I took one last look around my bedroom—the room I'd grown up in—and took in every last detail. My crocodile-tooth collection, my snakeskin presentation box, my books on earthworms and electric eels.

With one last look, I closed my bedroom door behind me, snuck out of the house, and made my way to the zoo.

Monday, March 16
Day 1 as a fugitive

Donny, Red, Georgina, and I piled into Donny's van late last night and sped away from the zoo under the cover of darkness. My stomach twisted in knots as I looked through the van window at Feral Zoo, slipping away into the distance. The thought that I might never see the zoo or my family again makes me feel sick. I'm leaving everything I love and heading into the unknown. If this is what it's really like to be a cryptozoologist—to put the protection of weird animals before your own happiness—then life is going to be harder than I ever thought it could be.

I couldn't speak as Donny's van ate up the miles. I didn't even ask where we were going or how we were going to survive—all I could think about was what I was leaving behind. Even Georgina seemed to sense that I was feeling bad— she sat on my lap and nuzzled her scaly body into me, looking up at me with her big gold eyes wide with worry.

After we'd been on the road for just over an hour Donny broke the silence. "We'll be there soon."

"Where are we going?" I finally managed to ask. I stroked Georgina, who had fallen asleep in my lap.

"Do you remember Jane the yeti?" Donny replied.

How could I forget—a furry giant nearly ten feet tall, yellow teeth as sharp as rusty daggers, and breath worse than the stench of rotting cabbages.

"Didn't Jane give you your first kiss?" Red teased from the front of the van.

"A kiss I'd rather forget," I replied grumpily. "Of course I remember Jane," I said to Donny, feeling my face flush red. "What about her?"

"We're going to her old yeti lair." Donny turned off the road and started driving through dark woodland. "It's been abandoned since she went back to Nepal with the other yetis. She won't mind us taking refuge there for the night."

The van pulled up in the woods and we all bundled out into the cold night. Georgina was still sleeping in my arms and I didn't want to wake her, so I carried her (she's getting really heavy!) through the trees until we reached the old yeti home. I was still feeling mega-bummed about leaving the zoo behind, but at least being here meant we had some kind of plan.

The entrance to the lair looked like a badger hole, and we took turns jumping down, landing with a thud in the cave beneath. As Donny and Red lit the cave up with torches it looked just as I remembered it—damp and bare and stinking of stale farts and rotten cabbage!

Yeti lairs = totally puke-worthy!

"We'll spend the night here," Donny announced, throwing three sleeping bags on the floor. I suddenly thought of my nice warm bed at home. I must be as bonkers as a bungee-jumping bear!

I curled up with Georgina inside a sleeping bag, trying to get warm. But yeti dens are FREEZING! I'd have been warmer if I'd snuggled up to a polar bear in the arctic!

After a few hours of broken sleep I woke to the smell of frying bacon. Donny was hunched over a small fire in the corner of the cave, cooking us breakfast, and Red was busy tapping away on a laptop. Georgina was curled up by Red's feet, surrounded by golden stones.

"Morning, snorer," Red said without looking up from the screen.

"I don't snore." I rubbed my eyes and yawned. "Is Georgina okay? Is that a new laptop?"

"So many questions!" Red shot back. "Yes,

Georgina's okay—she's been for a pee outside and managed to turn only one tree into solid gold, and, yes, it is a new laptop—seeing as Georgina turned the other one into a priceless sculpture."

"Breakfast is served!" Donny pushed a bacon sandwich into my hands. "We'll get on the road again as soon as we've eaten."

"You mean we're not staying here?" I asked, taking a bite of my sandwich.

"We need to keep moving," Donny replied, tucking into his own. "And we need to follow up a few leads Red's been looking into."

"I used a screenshot from security footage at the zoo to get a close-up of Mysterious Mistress X's face," Red informed me. "I've run that through the Internet, cross-referenced it with the databases of various security companies, national embassies, and banks, and managed to find out a bit more about Mysterious Mistress X."

"So you've spent most of the night hacking on your new computer?" I said. Red nodded. "What exactly have you found out?"

Red turned the computer screen around so I could read what was on it.

RECENT SIGHTINGS OF MYSTERIOUS MISTRESS X:

* Aboard a luxury yacht made from solid gold
* At golden mansions in Monte Carlo, Mystique, Mauritius, and Manila
* Shopping in Milan, Paris, London, and New York
* On a private jet made from gold

"It's pretty obvious what we have to do," Red grunted.

Er, is it?

"Mysterious Mistress X is only ever spotted in very glamorous places," Donny explained. "If we hide out in flea-infested rat holes, then we should be safe."

Can my life get any worse?

Not only have I left everything I love behind, but now I have to hide out in the scummiest places on earth!

"Well, staying here is a good idea then," I said, looking around at the moldy walls and cold stone floor of the yeti den.

"We can't risk standing still." Donny shook his head. "We need to keep running."

So that's what we've done . . . all day . . .

We've been driving up and down the country in Donny's van, only stopping to buy gas and food. We're spending the night sleeping on the edge of a stinking landfill. It smells one hundred times worse than the yeti den—Mysterious Mistress X will never look for us here! At least Georgina's having a great time flying around with all the pigeons who are diving for scraps of old food. The same old food that I have to sleep on!

Gross!

Don't get me wrong—I'm a normal kid. Some days I forget to put on clean socks and brush my teeth. But living on a landfill is beyond disgusting! After only one day on the run I'm not sure how much longer I can keep this up for . . .

Tuesday, March 17
Day 2 as a fugitive

We ate fish and chips on the sea front for lunch (after a morning of more driving around and trying to stop Georgina from turning the van to gold). Obviously we had to stand next to a sewage pipe while we ate . . . just to keep us under Mysterious Mistress X's radar.

Holding my nose with one hand, I took out my cell phone and switched it on for the first time since we'd left.

It buzzed with dozens of missed calls and texts, but before I could look properly Red snatched it out of my hands. "Sammy! What do you think you're doing?"

"Er, what does it look like?" I watched in horror as she threw my phone at the stinking sewage pipe, smashing it to smithereens. "What are YOU doing?" I shouted.

"Er, what does it look like?" she snarled back at me.

"Cell phones aren't safe, Sammy." Donny frowned. "Someone could use it to track us down. Remember how Mysterious Mistress X found us before—she put a trace on the computer you were using."

W.H.A.T?

No phones, e-mails, letters, texts, or anything? No way!

I had to find a way to get a message to Mom and Dad—just to let them know I was safe. They'd be going out of their minds with worry right now. I'd never run away like this before.

As if he knew what I was thinking, Donny said, "As soon as we're safe, Sammy, you can speak to them."

"But when will that be?" I said. "When we're buried underneath a heap of potato peelings and sleeping on toilet paper?"

"As soon as we have a plan to take down Mysterious Mistress X, obviously," Red said gruffly.

So we spent the rest of the day brainstorming as we drove.

These are just some of the (dumb) ideas we've dismissed so far . . .

* We target her private jet and melt the gold with a nuclear weapon
* We trick her into going for a swim in the sea so she sinks under the weight of her gold chains
* We keep running until we're all as gray as Donny

So, basically, we're as stuffed as a sausage. We have no plan to defeat Mysterious Mistress X and keep Georgina safe, and I may well never even SPEAK to my family again, let alone see them.

Wednesday, March 18
Day 3 as a fugitive

Three days without a proper shower (I smell like a trash can on a summer's day!), without a home-cooked meal, and without a proper bed to sleep in.

My life SUCKS LEMONS right now!

Even Georgina is getting grumpy—she accidentally turned Red's skull necklace to gold today. One step closer and she would have turned Red's head to solid gold! She's annoying, but I wouldn't want that to happen to her!

I was so homesick today I did something really, really bad. When Red was taking a nap and Donny was out getting us lunch I "borrowed" Red's new laptop and quickly checked my e-mails.

There were a dozen from Mom with various titles: "SAMMY FERAL, YOU COME HOME THIS INSTANT!," "YOU ARE IN SO MUCH TROUBLE, YOUNG MAN," "WE'RE WORRIED, SAMMY, COME HOME," and "COME HOME, SAMMY. YOU'RE NOT IN ANY TROUBLE."

Among the e-mails from Mom, one from Max caught my eye—the title read: "AMAZING PANDA DISCOVERY."

I quickly clicked on the e-mail and read it . . .

To: sammy@crypto.com
From: max@feralzoo.com

Sammy,

I hope you and Georgina are OK, wherever you are.

You'll never guess what—I've had an AMAZING panda breakthrough. I've discovered how they were able to turn

themselves invisible on Friday the
13th . . . with their snot.

Yes, panda snot has the power to make
things invisible. I discovered it by
accident—Su has a cold at the moment,
and every time he sneezes and his snot
lands on a stick of bamboo, it becomes
invisible.

You were right all along—pandas really
are very special creatures.

Stay safe.

Max

I showed the e-mail to Donny, and after he'd finished shouting at me for breaking his no-communication rule he said, "Well, it makes no difference. We can't go back to the zoo."

"But maybe the pandas can help us somehow?" I suggested.

"Stop fooling yourself, kid," Red grunted, seeming even grumpier after her nap. "Nothing can help us—we need to keep running."

"By now Mysterious Mistress X must know we're not at the zoo and that we've taken Georgina with us," I pointed out. "She'll be looking for us— maybe even in landfills and sewage pipes! The last place she'll look is back at the zoo. It might be the safest place for us right now!"

"Nice try, Sammy," Donny said, "but we're not putting anyone at the zoo in danger by going back there. Until we have a proper plan in place, we keep moving."

So that's what we're doing . . . still . . . moving, moving, moving . . .

There has to be some way that this panda breakthrough can help us. I mean, invisible snot is MASSIVE news! I can't help feeling we must be able to use it to keep Georgina safe and overpower Mysterious Mistress X once and for all . . .

Thursday, March 19
Day 4 as a fugitive

I'm writing this in the back of Donny's van as he drives up and down the freeway. I'm spending all my time thinking about my family and not about Mysterious Mistress X. Not good! How am I ever meant to come up with a plan to save Georgina if I can't think straight?

Maybe if I could just speak to everyone back at the zoo to let them know I'm okay, then I could think more clearly . . . I bet if I just quickly spoke to Max about panda snot then I might be able to come up with some kind of plan.

I don't care what Donny and Red say—I have to find a way to phone the zoo.

As soon as we stop for gas I'm going to make an excuse to sneak away—then I'm going to make the call . . .

6 P.M.

I seized my opportunity when Donny was filling the van with gas and Red had gone into the shop to buy snacks. I quickly bolted for the nearest payphone, slotted in my change, and dialed the zoo's number.

"Hello, you've reached Feral Zoo," came Dad's voice.

"Dad!"

"Sammy!" he gasped. "Are you all right? Where are you? Why did you run off like that? When are you coming home? Why didn't—"

Dad's voice was cut off by the sound of screaming in the background.

It sounded like Grace.

"Dad, is everything okay?" I asked, nervously. "That sounded like Grace—"

"Arghhhhh!!"

"Dad? What's going on?"

"Sammy," Dad said with panic in his voice. "Don't come back here—promise me."

"Why? What's happened?"

"There are soldiers here in the zoo . . . They're rounding everyone up . . . I can see them outside my office window . . . One of them is coming to my office door . . . He has a gun . . . Sammy!"

The sound of scuffling came down the phone. I heard Dad's voice shout something muffled and then another voice came on the line. "Sammy Feral."

It was a woman's voice. A strong Russian accent.

"Mysterious Mistress X," I whispered in horror.

"I'm pleased to be speaking to you, Sammy Feral," she said smoothly. "You have something I want very much."

"You can't have Georgina!" I said through gritted teeth. "You can do whatever you want but—"

"Whatever I want?" she chuckled. "I want to take every person and animal in Feral Zoo hostage, Sammy. I want to tie up your family and your pets . . . and if you don't come back here right away and give me Georgina, then I want to destroy everything you love."

The phone went dead in my hand.

Blood was pumping in my ears.

Suddenly my world had turned into a living nightmare and I could see no way out.

I dropped the payphone and sprinted back toward Donny's van. Georgina's face was pressed up against the window, steam from her large nostrils fogging up the glass. *"Mommy?"* she said as I came closer. *"What is wrong?"*

"Donny! Red!" I shouted.

Donny and Red appeared behind me, their faces full of concern. "What's going on?" Donny asked.

"I've just spoken to my dad," I said quickly. And before Donny could give me a blasting for using the phone, I said, "The zoo has been invaded by Mysterious Mistress X's army. Everyone is in danger. We have to go back."

"Sammy, it's not safe," Red said.

"I don't care about safe!" I shouted back at her. "I care about my family and I care about the zoo. I'm going back there, with or without you."

"We're in this together, Sammy." Donny nodded. "Let's go."

Friday, March 20

We raced down the freeway as quickly as the speed limit would let us. We HAD to get to Feral Zoo—we HAD to save my family!

By the time we arrived it was past midnight. Donny parked a few streets away from the zoo entrance. "Better that we get out here—we don't want anyone to see us coming."

With Georgina flying in low circles around us, we walked together through the pitch-black streets toward the zoo. All I wanted to do was run as fast as my legs would carry me, but Donny was right—we couldn't risk being seen. We had no weapons and no plan, and we were up against

Mysterious Mistress X and her ruthless army. The element of surprise was all we had on our side—well, that and the death-dealing smell of my armpits after five days without a proper wash!

When we were just around the corner from the main entrance Donny paused and turned to Red. "Do you have a mirror on you?" he asked.

Red reached into her back pocket and pulled out a small makeup mirror, which Donny used to look around the corner.

In the tiny reflection, lit only by the moonlight, I could see two soldiers pacing up and down outside the zoo, both armed.

"The zoo's being guarded by her army," Red whispered. "Do you think your family is still in there, Sammy?"

"I hope so," I replied.

I didn't want to think about the alternative— that she'd moved them somewhere I could never find them . . .

"Don't worry." Donny put his hand on my shoulder. "She won't harm them as long as we have Georgina. Otherwise what do we have to lose?"

I hated this.

I hated the thought of my family being in so much danger.

"We have no plan!" I said desperately. "We can't even get into the zoo. The minute we walk up to those soldiers they'll take us hostage too—they'll find Georgina and—"

"We can't let that happen," Donny said firmly.

"What are we going to do?" I asked.

"Psst!"

"Did you hear that?" I whispered.

"Psst!" came the noise again.

It was coming from a puddle on the side of the road.

I bent down to get a closer look and saw two bug-like eyes peeping out of the water.

"Wish Frog!" I gasped, scooping him up.

"I'm so pleased to see you, Sammy!" the little frog gulped. "The zoo's been taken over by—"

"We know," I said quickly. "We need to find a way to save everyone without handing Georgina over to Mysterious Mistress X. How did you get out?"

"The pandas sneezed on me and I managed to hop away without being seen," he replied.

The pandas! Of course! My brain must have

been frazzled by the constant smell of sewage in my nostrils—why didn't I think of it sooner?

"Listen closely," I said to everyone. "I have a plan. And it involves panda snot . . ."

6 A.M.

It was still dark when the wish frog and I left Donny, Red, and Georgina back in the van and ventured to the zoo.

It was time to put Plan Panda Snot into action! *"Mommy go?"* Georgina said as I was leaving.

"Yes, but I'll be back for you soon—I need you to be very, very well-behaved and sit here quietly with Donny and Red."

"Okay, Mommy," she said with an obedient smile.

The wish frog sat on my shoulder as I crept up to the zoo gates. I used Red's mirror to look around the corner, spotting the two armed guards pacing up and down.

"We creep in carefully," the wish frog reminded me. "The plan won't work if they catch us."

Slowly, when both guards were looking away, I crept out into the shadows and hid behind a tree. It was still dark and I knew the soldiers wouldn't be able to see me. They paced back and forth, and as soon as both their backs were turned again I slowly crept out from behind the tree and took cover behind a garbage can that was nearer to the zoo entrance.

I crouched, my knees aching from the awkward position, and the wish frog whispered in my ear, "Remember, the next move is the most crucial. You need to slip through the zoo gates and hide behind the ticket booth."

I only had a second to spring up from my hiding position the next time the guards' backs were turned. I ran toward the gates as silently as a stalking tiger.

Good job I'm still small enough to squeeze through the bars!

My heart pounded painfully in my chest as I ran toward the ticket booth and pressed myself up behind it. I closed my eyes and breathed a sigh of relief—I was inside the zoo!

"No time to relax, Sammy," the wish frog whispered. "Open your eyes . . ."

I peeped out from one eye and was horrified by what I saw.

Every animal enclosure had a soldier stationed in front of it—though luckily none of the soldiers were looking my way.

"How am I ever meant to get through the zoo unnoticed?" I said under my breath.

"Have faith, Sammy," the wish frog said calmly. "Remember why we're doing this—to save your family and protect Georgina."

The wish frog was right. Failure was not an option. I could not get caught. All I had to do was get to the Rare Animal Breeding Center . . .

* I picked up a plant pot and crept past the first set of guards
* I clung to the shadows as I snuck past the lions and tigers
* I crawled on all fours beneath the guards stationed high up in the monkey enclosure
* I tiptoed around the two-toed sloths and polar bears and the soldiers guarding them
* I writhed like a snake as I made my way around the reptile house

As I wiggled past the vultures and other large birds of prey I stuffed my pockets full of feathers that had fallen to the ground—all part of the plan.

The next stage was to set one of the vultures free . . .

I didn't have a key for the enclosure, but thank goodness Mom didn't notice when I once got a book about lock-picking out of the library! After only a minute of fiddling with the lock, the door to the vulture enclosure swung open.

Vinnie the vulture looked down at me, his beady eyes glinting in the moonlight. I stuck out my arm, just like Grace does when she's training the birds of prey, and Vinnie flapped down and perched on it.

I stroked Vinnie under his chin as I backed out of the vulture enclosure. This was the part of the plan that was crazier than a chameleon doing the cancan—I couldn't speak Vulture so I couldn't ask Vinnie to do what I needed him to do. I was just going to have to rely on my traditional zoo-keeping training.

With Vinnie on my arm and the wish frog hidden in my pocket among the vulture feathers (he was afraid to get too close to Vinnie!) I crept my way over to the Rare Animal Breeding Center.

There was a fat soldier slumped against the wall outside.

I took up a hiding spot behind a hedge. My eyes didn't leave the soldier as I silently counted to myself, One, two, three . . .

I threw my arm up into the air and Vinnie obediently launched himself high into the sky, squawking as he flew. The fat soldier looked up. His eyes locked on the huge vulture swooping toward him and his face flooded with panic. He aimed his gun—but before he had a chance to shoot, Vinnie pooped all over him.

Nice one, Vinnie! Talk about good luck—I'd never been so pleased to see a vulture poop!

The soldier fell to the ground blinded, his gun falling at his feet. I took my chance and ran out from behind the hedge toward the door of the Rare Animal Breeding Center. The handle turned in my hands and I quickly slipped inside. It was dark.

"There's no sign of my family at all," I whispered to the wish frog. "Where do you think Mysterious Mistress X is keeping them?"

"We can't worry about that now," the wish frog replied. "That's Donny and Red's job, once we've got what we came for."

What we came for = panda snot.

The pandas were asleep on their enclosure floor, chewed bamboo scattered around them.

I took a couple of vulture feathers out of my pocket and passed one to the wish frog.

He placed the feather under Su's nose and I held one under Cheng's.

We began to tickle the pandas.

Cheng sneezed so loudly she woke herself up. I managed to position myself in the path of the flying snot so I was splattered with it.

I looked down at myself. The parts of my body that had been hit by the snot—my hands and my arms—had turned completely invisible. Result!

"What do you think you're doing?" Cheng said loudly, as Su woke up with an extra-loud sneeze.

"We need your help," I said quickly. *"We need to collect as much snot as we can."*

"Why? And what makes you think we'll help you?" Su said grumpily. "Aren't you going to sing for us . . . or do a dance . . . or . . ."

"Feral Zoo is your home," I replied. This was no time for panda games! "You're happy here. You have enough food and water and people to care for you—all that will be taken away unless you help us fight off Mysterious Mistress X and save my family. And to do that we need your snot."

Cheng drew a deep sigh. "Very well, Sammy. There's an old bucket over there. You can use that to collect the snot in."

The wish frog and I spent half an hour helping Cheng and Su sneeze up as much invisibility snot as possible. Once the bucket was full, it was time to rock and roll. I smeared the sticky goo up my arms and legs, over my clothes and rubbed it into my face like sun cream. Then I covered the wish frog in it. I looked down at us and gasped—we were nowhere to be seen!

Oh man. Panda snot = AMAZING!

I tried to not get too excited and to stay focused on the plan—this was only the first step. I felt the wish frog hop onto my shoulder as I thanked the pandas.

Next step was to run as fast as I could through the zoo with the invisible bucket of panda snot, past the guards and back to the van.

I knocked gently on the van door.

"Who's there?" Red whispered nervously from inside.

"It's us," I replied. "We're invisible—we have enough snot for you all."

Donny and Red climbed out of the van and Georgina followed them.

"*Mommy?*" she asked.

"*I'm here, Georgina. You just can't see me.*"

"Quick—it's getting light." Donny pointed to the sun rising above the horizon. "We need to turn invisible so we can sneak back into the zoo with you."

Five minutes later everyone was dripping in panda snot and as invisible as air.

Donny quickly went over the last stage of the plan. "Red and I will sneak around the zoo searching for your family," he said. "Sammy, you go with the wish frog and Georgina to find Mysterious Mistress X."

"I know just where to look," I heard the wish frog say.

Wow—it was really confusing not being able to see anyone.

Once we were back in the zoo Donny and Red ran off to look for my family. "We'll start the search Backstage," Donny told me.

The wish frog said in my ear, "I think we need to look for Mysterious Mistress X in the amphibian house."

"Why?" I asked.

"Let's just say that Georgina isn't the only weird animal that woman's interested in."

The wish frog was right. As soon as I opened the door to the amphibian house I could hear Mysterious Mistress X's strong Russian accent.

"Now, which one of you pretty little frogs is going to grant me a wish?" she said. She was peering into a tank containing two dart frogs and poking them with a sharp stick. "Will it be you—" she poked one of them hard "—or you?" She poked the other.

"Frog cruelty!" I shouted loudly.

Mysterious Mistress X dropped the stick and spun around in shock. "Who said that?"

"You think you're so important just because you're rich," I said, walking toward her. I could feel Georgina flying next to my head, her warm breath on my neck. "But really you're just a nasty old woman who's cruel to animals."

"Where's that voice coming from? Who is that?" she shrieked.

I was standing right in front of her, but she couldn't see me. "You can't have the wish frog and you can't have Georgina."

"I always get what I want," she growled.

"There's something I want to ask you," I said, inching closer to her. "What does the X in Mysterious Mistress X stand for?"

Her eyes narrowed. "Sammy Feral, you might be invisible, but I know you're here in front of me, and I know you've brought my dragon back with you." She took a shaky step forward and held out her hands. "Come on, little dragon, come to Mommy. I won't hurt you, I promise."

"You're not her mommy," I said, feeling angry. "And if you won't tell me what your name means, then we have nothing left to talk about."

"Why don't we talk about how I tied your family up?" She grinned evilly. "Why don't we talk about how I'm going to tie your precious dragon up and she'll never see the sky again because I'm going to keep her in a dark, damp basement with only bats for company!"

"Georgina!" I shouted, so angry I wanted to scream. *"Fire, now!"*

"Fire now, Mommy? Inside?"

"Yes!" I shouted again. *"Fire now!"*

Georgina let out a small puff of smoke as she took a deep breath.

Mysterious Mistress X's eyes widened as she realized what was about to happen, but it was too late.

Georgina rose up into the air and let out a big fiery breath all over the wicked Mysterious Mistress X. I watched as her whole body turned to solid gold. Georgina had made her into a statue.

"Good girl, Georgina!" I said.

"Mommy pleased with me," I heard her reply. *"I do more to help Mommy?"*

"Yes, I need you to help me drag the golden statue outside."

Georgina's claws scraped at Mysterious Mistress X's golden head and I pushed from behind until we eventually got the statue outside the amphibian house. The sun was high in the sky and sunlight reflected off her golden head.

"Mistress?" said one of the soldiers who was standing nearby. "What's happened?"

I looked around for a way to clean the invisibility snot off Georgina, and spotted a hosepipe attached to an outdoor tap. I quickly ran over to it and turned the water on. I aimed the jet into the air and shouted, *"Georgina, fly into the water!"*

There was a splashing sound and suddenly

Georgina was flapping about in front of me, her golden wings glinting in the sunlight.

"It's a . . . It's a . . ." the soldier gasped.

"It's a dragon!" I shouted. "A dragon who will turn you to gold just like your mistress here unless you leave the zoo right now. *Georgina, fire, at the ground, now!*"

Georgina did as she was told and breathed fire all over the ground, quickly turning it to solid gold.

"So unless you want to end up a useless statue for the rest of your life, I suggest you round up the other soldiers and leave Feral Zoo—and if you ever come back, you'll be sorry!"

The soldier didn't need to be told twice.

He bolted away from us, his face as white as an arctic fox.

"Quickly!" I heard him shout to the other soldiers. "Release the prisoners and RETREAT! Mistress is defeated!"

As the soldiers began to flee I ran through the zoo, Georgina flying above me. I ran past the lions, past the giraffes and the buffalos, past the otters and the antelopes, all the way to the Backstage gates.

I burst into the Backstage yard to see my family and the other zookeepers tied up in one of the werewolf cages. They were being helped out of their chains by two invisible people.

"Georgina!" Grace called out. "Where's Sammy? Where's—"

"I'm here, Grace," I said, running up to the cage. "You can't see me because I'm covered in panda snot. Mysterious Mistress X is defeated and all the soldiers are leaving the zoo."

"You saved us!" Natty cried out.

I smiled. It felt good to know that my family was safe again.

"Sammy Feral, go and wash that panda snot off right away," Mom said, looking around for me. "I need to be able to see you."

Of course Mom wanted to see me.

I had saved the day—she'd want to hug me and shower me with praise and thank me for saving the zoo!

But Mom had other ideas. "You are in so much trouble, young man. I am never letting you out of my sight ever again!"

Saturday, March 21

"I don't care that all this time you've only been trying to keep Georgina safe. I don't care that you lied to us about having a dragon as a pet just to protect us. I don't care that you saved the day and rescued us all from the clutches of Mysterious Mistress X. You've missed a whole week of school, you haven't done your zoo chores and goodness only knows when you last had a wash—you smell worse than a pigmy goat with tummy trouble. You are grounded from now until you leave school!"

"Until I leave school?!" I said in horror as Mom

lectured me over the breakfast table. "But that's years away!"

"Well, you should have thought of that before you brought a dragon egg home, Sammy. After all, that is where this all began," Mom snapped back at me.

Honestly, you'd think my mom would be grateful that I saved her and the rest of my family, not to mention the zoo and Georgina from certain doom. Trust her to get hung up on the fact that I skipped out on my zoo chores.

"Your mother's right," Dad agreed, bending down to feed Caliban some of his leftover breakfast bacon.

Er, excuse me?

"But I'm training to be a cryptozoologist," I complained. "How can I learn what I need to if I can't even hang out with Donny and Red? And what about Georgina? She thinks I'm her mother—if she's going to be living at the zoo, then I need to visit her."

"Donny and Red can look after her," Grace suggested.

"They can't even speak Dragon!" I argued.

"Well, they'll just have to learn," Mom snapped back.

I don't think I've ever seen her this mad with me before.

I pushed my chair back and stood up to leave the kitchen table.

"Where do you think you're going, young man?" she said with narrowed eyes.

"To the zoo," I replied. "I have to catch up on my chores."

"That's right." Mom nodded. "But no going Backstage! I don't want you spending any more time around Donny and Red. This family has had enough yetis, werewolves, hell hounds, and dragons for a lifetime."

Mom might have had enough weirdness, but not me.

Even though I knew she'd feed me to the crocodiles if she found out I'd been Backstage, I had to find a way to visit Donny and Red. I had to explain to them that I wouldn't be helping out for a while—not until Mom calmed down. And I had to say goodbye to Georgina.

I managed to sneak through the Backstage gates without being noticed by the other zookeepers.

"Fancy a day of hanging out with the truth trout?" Donny asked me as I stepped through the Backstage office door.

"I can't," I said glumly. "I'm grounded for running away and I'm not even supposed to be Backstage. Ever again."

I noticed something golden twinkling in the corner of the room—it was the statue of Mysterious Mistress X. Donny was using it as a hat stand.

"Don't you want to spend as much time with Georgina as possible before she goes back to China?" Red asked.

What?!

"Georgina's going back to China?"

"Me go home to faraway land," Georgina said, flapping her wings as she perched on the shoulder of the Sammy Feral cardboard cutout. *"Me play with other dragons."*

I gulped back the tears that were threatening to spill down my face.

Somehow I thought that defeating Mysterious Mistress X and saving the day would be the end of all my problems. I didn't think Mom would be so mad at me. And I didn't think Georgina would be leaving the zoo.

"Why is she going?" I asked Donny, biting down on my lip. "And when?"

"Feral Zoo is no place for a dragon, Sammy," Donny said kindly. "Georgina's growing every day—she needs more space to fly around, and she needs to be with other dragons."

"We got this e-mail from Bruce this morning." Red floated her laptop into my hands.

To: donny@crypto.com; sammy@crypto.com; red@crypto.com
From: bruce@dragontemple.com

Dear Donny, Red, and Sammy,

Everyone at the Dragon Temple is so happy to hear that the evil Mysterious Mistress X is defeated! I'm glad that we trusted you and sent Georgina to you—you have done us proud.

Now that we know she is no longer in any danger, we will arrange for Georgina to come back to her rightful home—at the Dragon Temple.

I shall be in touch soon.

The Dragon Temple Guardians and the dragons themselves are in your debt for what you have done for us.

Thank you,

Bruce

Saturday, March 28

It's been over a week since Mysterious Mistress X was turned into a golden hat stand. And in that week I've had to do loads of extra homework and extra zoo chores to make up for running away. Thankfully, when Mom and Dad discovered that Georgina was leaving to go back to China, they let me spend some time with her each day.

The last week has been a mixture of happiness and sadness—happiness that I've been able to hang out with Georgina without the threat of Mysterious Mistress X hanging over us, but sadness that I know she has to leave and go back to China.

Bruce arrived at Feral Zoo today and we had a goodbye lunch for Georgina Backstage.

Everyone came—my family, Max, the wish frog, Mark, Donny, and Red—even the pandas joined in the fun. Mom had made sandwiches and cakes for the party and we played fetch with Georgina (she likes it when you throw a ball really high into the sky so she can fly after it). But I couldn't really enjoy myself. I just felt very sad.

"Sammy, you look as though the sun has stopped shining," the wish frog said as he sat on my shoulder and we watched everyone else play fetch.

"I'm sad because Georgina has to leave," I told him.

"But what a wonderful excuse to visit China one day." He smiled at me.

I looked down at the wish frog and smiled back.

He was right.

Just because Georgina was leaving Feral Zoo didn't mean I'd never see her again.

When it was time for Bruce and Georgina to leave, they began to cover themselves in panda snot for the long ride home.

"Are you going to ride Georgina all the way back to China?" Natty asked Bruce.

"Yes," he said, as he smeared invisible snot over his face. "But it's a long journey so we'll be making lots of stops along the way."

"*Georgina,*" I said, before she was completely covered in snot and I could still see her.

"*Yes, Mommy.*" She smiled at me.

"*I want you to know that you're the best dragon in the world. I wish you could stay here, but you'll be happier at the Dragon Temple. I'll miss you so much.*"

"*I won't miss you, Mommy,*" she said, still smiling. My heart sank. "*I have my other mommy with me.*"

I looked over to see Donny and Red smearing the Sammy Feral cardboard cutout with panda snot. "*You're taking that with you?*" I asked Georgina in surprise.

"*Me not go anywhere without my mommy.*" She looked contented.

I reached over and gave Georgina a massive hug, smearing panda snot on myself so I had small blotchy invisible patches all over me.

Soon Bruce and Georgina were completely invisible and all we could hear was the flapping of Georgina's wings as she rose into the sky and the sound of Bruce's voice as he called down at us, "Thank you and goodbye!"

"Wow, I'm really going to miss Georgina," Grace said, wiping a tear from the corner of her eye.

"Me too," I whispered. "But as soon as I can I'm going to China to visit her."

"Not before you've swept out the skunks and fed the penguins," Mom said sternly.

"And I've had a report of unicorns that need some help," Donny said.

I looked over at Mom, sure she'd say there was no way I could go hunting unicorns with Donny. But instead she just sighed and said, "If Donny needs your help, then I won't stand in your way."

I lurched forward and hugged her. "Thanks, Mom," I whispered.

"Come on then, Sammy," Donny called over his shoulder as he walked toward the Backstage offices. "Unicorns are vicious things—we need to act fast."

"Coming!" I shouted back.

So one adventure ends and another is about to begin.

I guess that's the story of my life— one weird adventure after another.

I wouldn't change a thing.

Sammy ☺

Don't miss Sammy Feral's other *WEIRD* adventures!